I0642766

Sister Séance

Aimee Parkison

KERNPUNKT ⬤ PRESS

Copyright © 2021 by KERNPUNKT Press

All rights reserved. This book or any portion thereof may not be reproduced or used in any manner whatsoever without the express written permission of the publisher.

Cover Art: An edited still from the 1922 film *Dr. Mabuse, the Gambler,* in the public domain
Book Design: Jesi Buell
Editors: Patrick Parks and Jesi Buell

ISBN-13 978-1-7343065-1-4

KERNPUNKT Press
Hamilton, New York 13346

Dumb Supper

Kora (serving)

Valerie Usherwood

Maggie Usherwood

Invisible Guest

Table

Dr. Ian Burrows

Viv Hayden

Chris Datchery

Aria Hayden

Mason Turner

Florence Green

Henry Turner

Hattie Grove

Jerry Rickett

Grace Hayden

Major General Sampson Redlaw

Belle Hayden

Nick Dalton

Ruby Turner

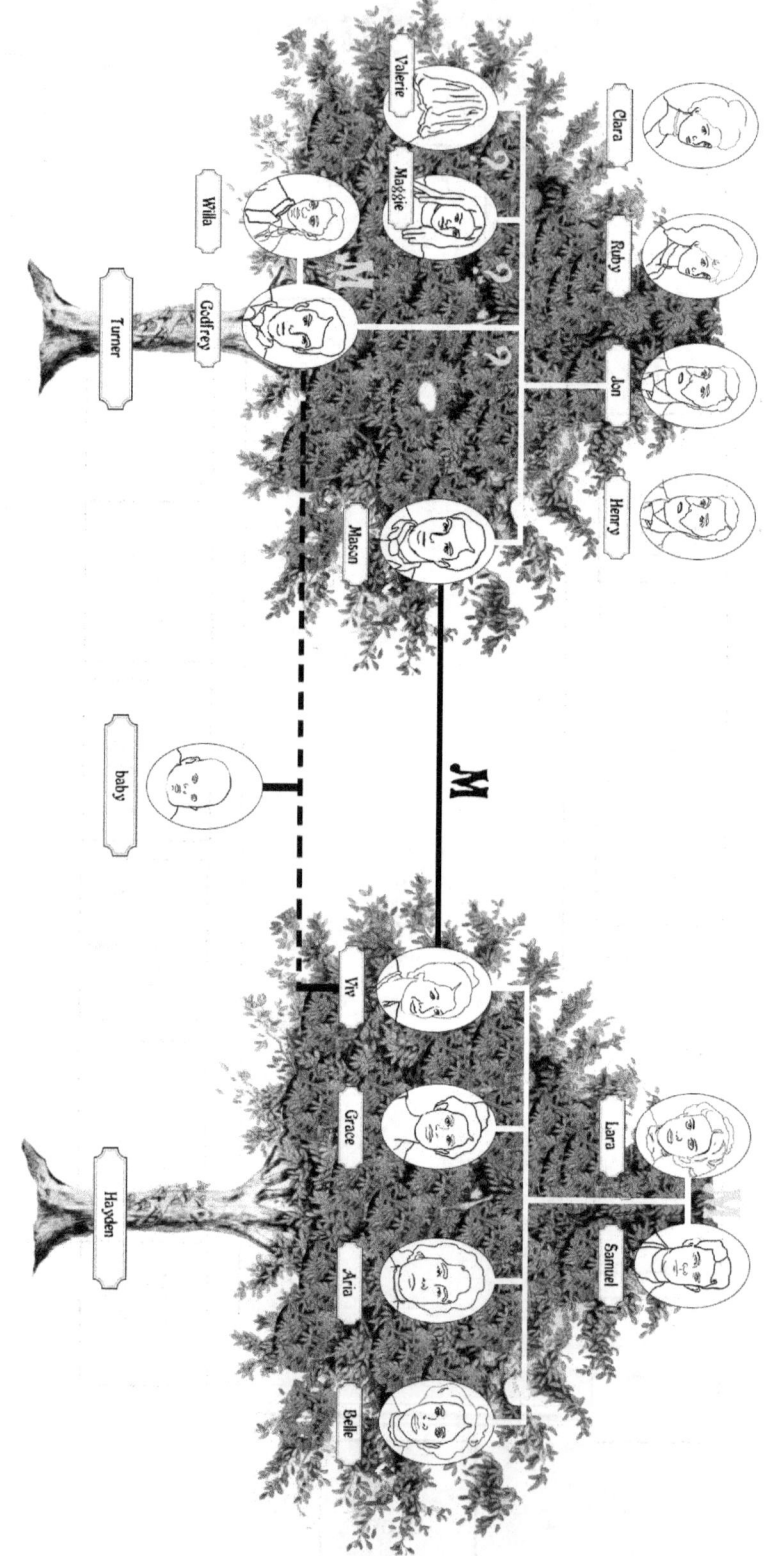

Part
I.

1.

Viv used her cameras to start anew after the war. In Concord, people appreciated her skill. A seasoned photographer, she inventoried pristine cotton paper while imagining what she could accomplish with salt, egg white, and sunlight. Viv was grateful glass-plate negatives were extremely light sensitive, making exposure times speedy. She often relied on albumen silver prints with the delicate lucidity of daguerreotypes and the vast reproducibility of paper prints.

After arranging chemical baths and a portable darkroom, Viv set up her cameras in front of benches upstairs in Miss Turner's boardinghouse. Awaiting the prize-winning couple from the costume contest, Viv intended her photographs of the couple to be a lasting memento of Concord's 1865 Halloween Triumph.

What type of costumes would win the prize? Viv wondered. Town Hall was probably bustling with couples parading in disguise before an audience of contest judges and admiring crowds.

The boardinghouse felt empty with so many people at the Town Hall, which hosted the costume contest followed by public conversations. After these events, small groups would scatter to parlors of private houses, hayrides, and dinner parties.

The most anticipated dinner party of Halloween was the dumb supper hosted by Miss Ruby Turner inside the boardinghouse. Several couples from the costume contest would be guests, and Viv would feast among them without speaking.

The dumb supper required conversation without words, so the guests must communicate in silence. Silence was supposed to attract the presence of a spirit of a deceased person, a ghost. If rumors were to be believed, an "invisible guest" would sit at an empty chair at the dinner table. This was done in jest, though Spiritualists believed. Spiritualists were growing in number because many families had lost loved ones to sickness and the war. Those in the deepest mourning were trying to reconnect with loved ones they had lost and Spiritualism provided a way. At the dumb supper, believers and nonbelievers would take vows of silence.

Downstairs, door hinges screeched like mating owls before rude footsteps thundered up the boardinghouse's central stairs with dry wood steps weeping in brittle protest.

"Up here, I'm ready," Viv called to shrill laughing voices in the hallway.

The baby leapt inside her. Viv smiled. No one could be allowed to know why. She hadn't confessed her circumstance to her sisters or anyone in Concord.

Disguised in elaborately carved bone masks, a couple tiptoed through Viv's room. Shaken by their lack of courteous introduction, Viv stared at the bone masks framed in long wild wigs of horse hair. Accented with deep hollow eye sockets dark as shadow, the masks exposed real teeth in wide obscene smiles. The smiling masks presented a special problem, disturbing Viv's plan. No polite person smiled in photographs. It was considered improper.

"Would you like to remove your masks so I can capture your faces?" Viv asked.

The man shook his head. His wild wig unfurled to the hardwoods.

"Well," said Viv. "Your masks are terrifying because of the way they're grinning."

Instead of removing their masks, the couple approached the cameras silently. The man positioned himself and the woman held his hand as they sat together, posing on a bench. Viv took their picture, and the couple left without thanking her, removing their masks, or saying goodbye.

Viv brushed her fingertips across her belly, a protective gesture to reassure her unborn and herself.

Alone in the room again, Viv took a deep breath and gazed out the window at autumn leaves falling toward the woods. Making her way past chemical baths and toner, she whispered, "It's fine. We're safe. No one knows you're here."

"Viv?" Miss Ruby Turner called from behind the doorway.

Viv jumped, trying to disguise her surprise.

"Is everything alright, dear?" asked Miss Ruby Turner, her thick hair falling out of its braid.

"Yes," said Viv. "Miss Turner, you only startled me."

"Sorry, dear. I just wanted to let you know the prize-winning couple from the costume contest are downstairs, waiting for their portrait."

"Are you certain?"

"Oh, yes. They've just arrived. The most adorable cat and mouse you've ever seen. Wait until you see their furry ears and tails."

"Really? If you're sure," said Viv, "send them up. I'm ready."

Whom had she photographed in the grinning bone masks? Viv shivered, not from cold. Had someone pulled a prank on her, or was it just a misunderstanding? She had no idea and no time to consider.

Viv prepared her cameras again.

Two teenagers, a pimply boy and a pudgy girl with long golden hair, peeked into the room. The girl was dressed as a cat, and the boy was dressed as a mouse. Neither wore a mask. They sat on the bench together, having just announced their engagement. Viv's camera caught the mouse gazing at the cat with tender eyes.

"She caught me," the boy said, laughing, before Viv instructed them to sit very still for the camera. She wanted to take more than one photograph, to capture the sweetness and light in their gazes because she could tell how they loved each other.

Seeing how sweet they were reminded Viv that less than five years ago, she was innocent like them.

* * *

Viv grew up in a house full of jewels, though she hated wearing jewelry. Wearing jewelry reminded her of women in chains—ghastly stories she had read in newspapers. For this reason, she much preferred capturing impressions to wearing gems.

Before the war, she stole her mother's jewelry. She had no remorse about stealing because she thought she could use the stolen jewelry to save others while her mother, Lara, attended silly little séances with Spiritualists.

* * *

Now that Viv was living in Ruby's boardinghouse and Viv's mother was gone forever, Viv wondered if Ruby really believed she was meeting Viv and her sisters for the first time. Viv had photographs of Ruby and their mother in Boston—or at least photographs of the woman who looked like Ruby. Cameras being so rare, custom made, enormous and expensive, photography required a good deal of patience as well as knowledge of toxic chemicals for the printing process. Viv learned to take photographs by practicing with a camera at home—the camera her father paid a professional to build just for her and to teach her to use.

In those days before she lost her mother, when she was a sheltered child sucking on peppermints, Viv shivered at wintery windows. She was imagining all the people in the city blanketed in snow, yet the Hayden mansion, bathed in cozy gaslight, was kept well heated, stocked with coal, lit with many hearth fires and wood-burning stoves.

Wrapped in gleaming fur shawls, Viv waited for the maids to retire to the moonlight, to drop her father's discarded newspapers into the bin near the hearth. Not allowed to read newspapers, Viv had to make sure no one noticed. Biding her time, during the final moments of daylight, Viv stared out the parlor's foggy picture windows at workers ending their long days, walking home. Streets whitened. Fat snowflakes fell, twisting in swirls of wind. Carriages trudged through the drifts where the breath of horses drew pale mist. School boys, teenagers like Viv, darted through the streets of Boston while hurling hard-packed snowballs. Viv groaned, having little patience for boys. Paying attention to men, she wondered if any were abolitionists of the Underground Railroad.

Everything changed for her in the winter of 1861, a time of Fugitive Slave Law and the Bloodhound Law. Viv was about to leave her life behind, months before the Great Rebellion, which would one day be known as the Civil War. A sense of growing injustice flowed through Viv's veins, pulsing through her heart and mind. She was about to do something none of her sisters would ever do. She knew better than to tell a soul.

Viv kissed her mother on the cheek, so her mother would leave her alone with the discarded newspapers. Her mother smiled and then stomped toward the kitchen, corsets straining, her silk dress swishing as her wooden heeled shoes clomped on the hardwoods.

Oh, Mother, Viv thought, *how I betray you*. Viv had no way of knowing that once she left home, it would be for years. She would only briefly return to see her mother and father again at the end of the war, before she ended up living with her mother's friend Ruby, who took pity on her and her sisters after their parents' unexpected departures. Because what she read in the newspapers disturbed and motivated her, Viv took care not to rustle the pages. Viv clipped articles her parents didn't want her to read about Reverend Henry Ward Beecher of Plymouth Church. After hiding the clippings in her scrapbook, she folded the pages so they appeared untouched when the maids burned them in the fire.

Viv had never had a beau, never started courting. Not interested in boys, she was fascinated by photography, news, and men. She wanted to run away from home to find Reverend Beecher. She wanted to bid at the mock auctions of enslaved people at Plymouth Church. Men like Beecher excited Viv and made her nervous, especially at night in her dreams, where she always ended up at Plymouth Church, fighting the crowds, attempting to get closer to the pulpit.

In her dreams, Beecher stood on a stage next to an impossibly handsome gentleman in chains. Beecher's voice boomed in the church's enormous theater, seating thousands of Christians. Beecher was speaking in the voice of an auctioneer, and Viv began bidding—wondering if a girl could save a man.

Upon waking, Viv always smiled at the oddness of her recurring dream, wondering what it meant. Even as a teenager, she knew it had to be kept secret. She wondered if Beecher's infamous church was auctioning only women and girls.

"Viv, Viv," her sisters called from Aria's room, down the hall.

Belle ran to Viv. Belle in blue velvet, eyes dazzling, donned their mother's sapphire necklace with matching bracelets and earbobs. She was a little lady, rather pale and petite, sickly. Whenever someone close to the Haydens died, mourners brought the hair of the deceased to Belle, who sculpted flowers out of the strands. Viv winked at Belle, while making a mental note to steal the sapphires that night. Those sapphires, Viv realized, could buy someone's freedom.

If Viv was breaking laws and violating the trust of her family, she thought it for a good cause. No matter what happened, she counted on her father to forgive her.

"Viv," Grace called. "Why aren't you trying on necklaces with us?"

"Just a minute," Viv called out, closing her scrapbook

on Rev. Beecher's solemn face. Pearls, she realized, would also do well at the auction, as would her mother's jet, gold chains, and dangling rubies. Her mother didn't really care for diamonds anyway, and her sisters cared too much.

Viv knew she could do anything, even steal jewelry from her mother and coins from her father, and her family would always forgive her. They treated her like a baby, indulging her whims. If they had their way, they would cage her forever, trapping her inside their mansion with its red velvet curtains.

"Viv," Belle called. "Do you want to try Mother's emeralds or her topaz?"

"How about the rubies?" Viv asked.

"Grace has them and the yellow diamond pendant."

Viv frowned. Grace always chose the yellow diamond and the rubies to borrow from their mother. Trying not to laugh, Viv realized how upset Grace would be when she noticed them missing. In time. All in good time.

"Are you upset with me?" Grace asked, her light-colored hair piled high, braided and wrapped like a crown. She stood before the oval mirror, gazing at herself and stroking the yellow diamond glinting at her slender neck.

"Not at all," Viv said, grinning. "Why on earth should I be?"

"Viv never cares about jewelry," said Aria. "Why should she? Her hair shines brighter than any jewel. Like flames."

Viv smirked at Aria. Her disdain for jewelry had nothing to do with her hair. She didn't want a life of luxury or of privilege. She wanted to make a difference, to make the world a better place. In her heart, she knew slavery was a crime against all humanity. She wanted to help Rev. Beecher fight it. There was no way for her to do that inside her father's mansion, where she ate elegant meals with family, photographed her sisters and guests, or stood at the windows to stare at carriages paused on snowy street corners. Perched high above it all, framed in the jeweled windows, she watched the world go by, waiting for a chance to be part of it.

Plotting her escape, Viv knew she had to act fast, that night, and to take very little—only cash, jewelry, silverware, coins, food, and matches. Only what would be easy to take quickly, without waking her family, especially her mother, who had a curious hobby—weeping behind closed doors and collecting her tears in glass vials.

Lachrymatory, it was called. Because a fashionably grieving lady collects her tears in a bottle, a lot of women wept that way, but few kept their mourning such a secret. In all her life, Viv never knew who or what her mother mourned for and this was one of Viv's greatest regrets after she lost her. She still possessed her mother's lachrymatory bottle, though the tears inside had long ago escaped into the air. When mourning the loss of loved ones, women like Viv's mother collected their tears in bottles with special stoppers that allowed the tears to evaporate. When the tears had evaporated, the mourning period would end. Whenever Viv's mother was alone, she often started to cry, and Viv never knew why, though she found the tear vials misty. It was easy to steal from her mother because her father bought her mother jewelry every time her mother cried and her mother didn't pay attention to the jewelry, only to her tears.

That night she betrayed her family and changed her life forever, Viv waited for her family to fall asleep. She listened through the vents for their breathing. In the dark of bedcurtains, she pretended to be asleep, though she was wide awake with her eyes closed.

Lighting a single candle, she crept to her enormous camera propped on its stand. She kissed it goodbye, weeping softly for every photograph she had taken and all the photographs she wanted to take. Would she ever see her camera again? Few girls knew how to operate cameras or could afford them, and yet her tutor and her father had promised she had a rare talent for photography. Her father had gifted the camera to her and had it custom made. It was a luxury too large to carry and would have to be left behind. This pained her, though she knew it was silly. What good would her hobby do her now?

Viv packed a suitcase with jewelry and money. Hiding her bright red hair under her father's dark cap and wearing his casual clothes, which were several sizes too big for her, she wanted to look like a boy. Into a large pack, she squirreled away a canteen, several loaves of bread, six pounds of deer jerky, five apples, and her father's coin collection. Before sneaking out the back door of the house, she wrapped scarves around her face, only her eyes peeking through the knit. Outside, on the near-empty night streets, she trudged through the snow. Moving from gaslight to gaslight, she was on her way to the train station.

She slept on the train, still dressed as a boy.

When the train finally arrived at Brooklyn, she asked the first woman she met for directions. It was easy to find Plymouth Church. Everyone knew where it was, but Viv was surprised to discover the church a brick building of simple design, reflecting the Puritan ethic of plain living.

On the church steps, congregants were handing out pamphlets on Beecher's sermons, counseling disobedience to the Fugitive Slave Law, declaring the rights of humanity were above the Constitution, and encouraging all to join the Underground Railroad to fight the Bloodhound Law.

Viv snuck inside the church, found a broom closet, and hid. With so many people coming and going, it was easy to disappear among them. Laying low, she felt ready to join the auctions in the giant theater surrounding the pulpit. The church's theater offered seating for nearly 3000 people. Viv slept, dreaming of the auctions. She beheld the promise of her mother's jewels gleaming by the sliver of light beneath the closet door.

On Sunday morning, hearing the thunder of shoes passing by in the hall outside the closet, Viv shuddered against the door. She heard many voices, speaking in anticipation of the auction of enslaved women and girls. The mock auction! It was meant to free captive people by raising funds from the congregation.

Slowly, Viv opened the closet door, pushing it, forcing it against the gathering crowd on their way to the theater. Falling into the hall, she was absorbed by the crowd of Christians. Following them, part of the flow of hundreds, she was overjoyed as they led her to the theater. "Beecher, Beecher," they whispered, as if the reverend were a god. Viv felt chills running down her back as she clutched the bag of her mother's jewelry.

Beecher strode onto the stage, and a hush fell over the theater of thousands. "Here, come here, my child, come," he called from the pulpit in the center, coaxing a girl who stood off stage. Slowly, a little girl in a white dress, shivering, covering her mouth with her hands, approached the pulpit—a girl with pale skin and dark tight neat curls flowing down white ruffles of her sleeves. Beecher gently led the girl to the pulpit, whispering kindly in her ear, fatherly, as if to pacify and reassure her. When she stopped shaking long enough for him to hold her hand, a strange change overcame his face. Suddenly, Beecher began to yell to the crowd, talking about the girl as if she weren't human but an animal, praising her beauty and then calling out in the voice of an auctioneer. Bid calling the cattle rattle for the girl, Rev. Beecher spoke at an incredible pace. The girl began to weep as the reverend quoted the current price, sixty-five dollars, before calling the asking price to outbid.

"Can I get a $70 bill for a nice young one, would I get a $75 bill for a girl so sweet?" Beecher called as the little girl cowered beside him. "Never been touched. Would I get an $80 bill for a pure child? Would I get a $90 bill for a little tiny darling who will do everything you command? Would I get a $100 bill for this little doll, this tiny woman? Somebody bid now on this pretty one. Make it 180 for one fine lady one day. Can I have a 200 for a girl who will be a woman in time? How about a 210 for a child who can have a child one day? 210, 210, 210? 215, 215? Here! 220? 2-can I get a 2-20? Thank you, sir. That's a 2-20. Look at her pretty eyes, her little hands? Her mouth, can I hear a 225 for the mouth on this child? A 230 for the pretty eyes? 230,

230? Now, 235, 240?"

When Viv finally rushed toward the stage, shoving her way through the crowd, she found the reverend even more attractive in person than his photograph in the newspaper. Reverend Beecher commanded the pulpit with his booming voice, neat attractive features, thick well-groomed hair, hooded eyes, and stylish tailored suit. His energetic auctioneer's voice invigorated ladies who tittered and then began to weep in their husbands' arms.

Viv was soon caught up in the wave of outrage as another frightened girl was led onto the stage—this one a teenager, Viv's age. Beecher, talking about the girl and what would happen when she was sold by traders who really auctioned enslaved people, stirred the indignation of thousands. It was as if his voice could leer. But it was all an act, a performance to draw a correct reaction of outrage from the crowd, who paid and paid. His charisma overwhelmed Viv. The bidding began as the girl stood in silent terror staring at the crowd.

"Five, 10, 15, 20. Here, here, there, I have 35. 45? Five-five, would you bid 10 more? Ten, would you bid 15? One fifteen, one, one, twenty. Do I hear a one twenty for her, a girl not yet twenty? Do you think a hundred forty? Two? Was that a two? A wife who will do whatever you want to do and you won't even have to marry her. 210? Now 215. Thank, you, sir. Sir, sir, would you bid a 2-20?"

Casting her mother's pearls into offering plates and waving sapphires high on several Sundays, Viv thought she understood what the reverend was doing. She had been caught up in the outrage when children were sold but the auctions raised questions unsettled in Viv's mind.

Somehow, what was happening didn't make sense, even though Viv fully supported the abolitionists' cause. At night, hiding in the broom closet, she couldn't keep from wondering where were the enslaved men and why wasn't Beecher bringing them to his crowds to free? If Beecher's pulpit had become a prison, it was because the women and girls he saved were beautiful, she started to think. Maybe their beauty put them in more danger.

But weren't there any captive men in similar danger?

Viv slowly began to realize the church wouldn't encourage such questions and perhaps wouldn't tolerate a young woman asking them. She tried to seek out other women in the church, to ask for food and to see if the women had similar questions.

Beecher strode past Viv. She spun to stare. Her father's cap fell off her head. She gasped. Beecher turned back and paused to examine her red curls, long and finally free, cascading down her shoulders in waves.

Beecher admonished Viv, saying it wrong for her to be dressed as a boy. He procured dresses for her, donated by caring members of his congregation, and a kindhearted elder lady offered to let Viv stay in her house.

During tea at the old woman's house, women whispered to Viv that Beecher's church was one of the most active stations on the Underground Railroad, the path escaped enslaved people took to Canada. Viv knew death or imprisonment could be the consequence, but she wanted to start working for Beecher and his team of abolitionists.

Plymouth Church had its own stationmasters and conductors, who helped organize runaways' passages north. Pale-skinned enslaved women called "concubines" were often rescued by Rev. Beecher, who warned of high prices paid for them on the auction block and on the plantation, where the "one-drop rule" governed all. Rumors traveled fast to Viv and the rest of the congregation's women.

Viv was terrified that she, too, might be sold, though her eyes were green and her hair was flame red curls. Wearing a borrowed charcoal velvet dress, she imagined herself and her sisters in chains, being sold at auction. Just then, Beecher marched into the room. All the women's eyes moved over him as he strode to Viv, grasped her hands, and led her out of the parlor, into the drawing room, with the men, for a talk.

"Viv," Rev. Beecher said, motioning to all the men in the room, "can you even imagine what men would do after they have bought women and own them?"

"No," Viv whispered.

"If you're in the wrong place at the wrong time, it could happen to you or your sisters. Most Southerners don't want us to know all women are at risk."

He asked Viv many questions about herself and her family and became especially interested when she mentioned her ability to take photographs.

The reverend claimed wealthy Southern families like the Turners of Tennessee wanted to keep the condition of their enslaved people a secret, but Beecher said the church wanted to expose such secrets with new methods in photography.

"Turner?" Viv asked. "I know that name." She thought of her mother's childhood friend, Ruby.

"Isn't that so?" Beecher asked the elders in the church library. The elders spoke of Beecher's hope of infiltrating plantations with undercover abolitionist photographers, to document the lives of enslaved people.

"So far, this scheme has failed. To make it work, I need images of what goes on at the Turner plantation behind closed doors," Beecher said at the secret meeting. "When I met you, Viv, I knew the Lord had answered my prayers. You, girl, are our secret weapon!"

"Me?" asked Viv, afraid to look anyone in the eye.

The reverend introduced Viv to the conductors who ran his railroad. They asked if she was to be one of the spies.

As she learned more about the railroad, Viv recalled watching the most famous auction, the mock sale of a little girl named Pinky. Pinky, a pretty pale girl with long hair and Caucasian features. Since it only took one drop of African blood to keep a girl in slavery, Pinky was not free until Rev. Beecher sold her by mimicking how the auctioneer would sell her, leering, implying what her fate would be.

Women fainted into the arms of their husbands, fathers, and brothers at the little girl's humiliation. Raising an ungodly sum to free her, Christian men emptied their wallets, and Christian women began removing their jewelry and throwing it onto the stage and into offering plates.

Giving away a lovely opal ring, the last of her mother's jewels, Viv silently cursed that she didn't have a camera with her. Reverend Beecher removed the opal ring from the offering plate, placed it on the Pinky's finger, and said, "With this ring, I do wed thee to freedom."

Viv gasped, along with the other women, as Pinky gazed at the ring on her finger and smiled. The congregation cheered.

Beecher called out. "Is she not your sister?"

"Yes," Viv screamed.

Beecher wailed. "Is the price too high for your daughter's freedom? Look at her! Beauty comes so cheap!"

"No child should be in slavery, let alone a child like this. She could be your niece. She could be your sister. Your sister's child. Yours!" After this speech, Beecher passed the collection plate, again, and Viv felt sad she had nothing else to give.

Rev. Beecher held several more "auctions" to buy the freedom of enslaved girls, selling them in the church to rescue them from slavery. Not long after one of these church auctions, Beecher invited Viv into his library and showed her a painting of a young man, the most beautiful man she had ever seen.

"How would you like to rescue him?" Beecher asked.

"He's a gentleman. Isn't he?" asked Viv.

"Can't a gentleman be enslaved?" Beecher asked.

"I never imagined someone like him."

"Too bad this is only a painting. I would like to see a photographic likeness. I would photograph him myself, if I had the chance."

"You!"

"But, alas, I'm not a photographer."

"How could I save him? He's a gentleman, isn't he?" asked Viv.

"A gentleman. But enslaved. Photograph him, if you like, and I'll see what I can do to raise the funds to set him free, but what I really want is to buy the freedom of his younger sisters, twins. They are the ones whose photographs we need most of all."

"What's his name?"

"Godfrey Turner. His brother, Mason Turner, is the plantation owner's sole heir. Mason has requested my help to free Godfrey and his sisters, twins so young, so innocent, so very ladylike and girlish in their charms, so helpless and artless, even a single photograph would be enough to spark abolitionist outrage to spread like fever."

"But how?"

"Use your talents, Viv, and your beauty."

"But, Reverend, how?" asked Viv.

"Become one of the Turner family. Marry Mason Turner."

"Marry him?"

"As his wife, you'll be in the perfect position of trust to use your skills as a photographer to take photographs of the twins, as evidence, to send to me, so I can show the church."

This was how Viv first realized Rev. Beecher had struck an unholy bargain to give her to Mason Turner. Mason and Godfrey were secretly working with Rev. Beecher to free the young twin sisters, but Rev. Beecher claimed the men needed her help.

"How could my photographs help?" asked Viv, taking in the story the reverend told.

"We could circulate certain types of photographs and paintings in the North and in the South," said Beecher. "Photographs are valuable to our cause when they show us what makes us uncomfortable, what we don't want to see. We are all the same family. Understand, Viv? I need photographs to prove that point to citizens who are not yet on our side but wavering."

"I guess," she said, still wondering why he didn't care to help males and what could be done for Godfrey.

"But are you willing to give yourself to Mason Turner for the cause?"

"If I must."

Beecher said, "You'll soon be a good Southern lady with the best camera money can buy."

That evening, over dinner, Viv imagined cameras and adventures. Her fantasies of Godfrey deepened as Beecher told her tales of women in New Orleans known as "fancy gals." Where were the "fancy men?" She wondered.

* * *

"Miss Viv? Miss?"

The young couple dressed as cat and mouse were watching Viv with expressions of growing concern as she emerged from her framing closet, where she dried prints in the absence of light. The couple began staring at her in the most curious manner. "Excuse me. Miss Viv, are you quite alright?" the boy asked. "Do you need anything else from us?"

"I'm sorry?" Viv asked. "What do you mean?"

"Will we have our portrait now?" asked the girl. "My mother would love to have it for our parlor wall."

"Oh," said Viv. "I can't show you until the photograph is finished. It must be dried, exposed to light, fixed in a chemical bath, and then set with toner, before being framed. In about a day, it should be ready, framed and presentable. Would that be alright? I'm afraid I can't work any faster since I must prepare for the dumb supper tonight. Of course, my work will be interrupted by festivities in this house. It will be quite impossible to accomplish much else for the rest of the day, or night."

"Yes," said the girl. "We understand. We've been invited."

"Wonderful," said Viv. "I hope to see you at the dumb supper. I'll deliver your portrait after I've finished, in no more than two days' time. But where should I call on you?"

"My family residence is Blankenship House," said the girl. "I'll tell Mother to expect you."

The cat reached out to the mouse. The young couple entwined fingers while holding hands. Viv bid them farewell, congratulating them for winning the costume contest. Whispering and giggling, the cat and mouse began descending the creaking stairs of the boardinghouse as Viv wondered if they would spend all day in costume or change and then dress in costume again before the party.

2.

Willa braced against the wind. Church bells chimed brightly through Sleepy Hollow. In woods that cushioned Concord, autumn leaves glowed golden red. Fighting the chill of orchard air and walking the mist in amber sunlight, Willa thought of Viv with sadness. When they lived at the plantation called Twin Oaks, Godfrey couldn't escape Viv's caresses without risking his life and Viv never understood what she had done or how she had harmed Willa.

Willa and Godfrey were not brother and sister, as Viv believed. Godfrey loved Willa tenderly in the shadows to protect their secret union.

Now, Viv was the one pretending. As far as Willa knew, Viv was hiding her pregnancy, carrying Godfrey's child, and thinking that Godfrey was in love with her.

If rumors were to be believed, Viv was in Concord, staying in the women's boardinghouse. Willa had promised Godfrey to find Viv and the boardinghouse because the unborn child was part of Godfrey and innocent of the things its mother had done. Godfrey wanted to be a father to the child, despite the way it came into the world. He wanted Willa to be the child's mother, if Viv would let the child go, and Willa desperately wanted that for herself, Godfrey, and the child. If Godfrey lived, he would be a father. If Godfrey died, the child would be all that was left of him.

Willa inhaled the cozy scent of distant hearth fires. Chimneys smoked. The sky brightened over nearby farmhouses. She crept toward Walden while longing for a home. Traveling on foot, Willa had escaped the tobacco plantation and now had no place to rest. She was as homeless as she was free, traveling far to escape the South and its night riders. She left her home when a group of men in Tennessee, pretending to be ghosts of Confederate soldiers, joined the Klan. In the guise of ghost Confederates, they haunted freedmen, hunting freedwomen by night, throwing freedmen over bridges, burning men in trees, and stealing the love of her life, her Godfrey. The Klan, folks said, would not be in Concord. It was once a stop on the Underground Railroad. Too many abolitionists and Union soldiers lived there to tolerate the Klan.

Walking near Concord River, Willa stumbled upon a young woman crouched beside an old elm. The young woman was clinging to roots knotted like elderly fingers reaching through earth. Willa thought of darting into the trees to hide, then saw blood.

The woman crawled deeper into the woods.

Willa envied and pitied the woman for her condition, which Willa knew she would never have to face. Perhaps knowing she was unable to have children made her sensitive to the condition of pregnant girls and women, especially those who were in danger. Because she learned how to midwife at a young age, she had welcomed many babies into the world. She was the first to hold these babies while comforting their mothers. One of the most gifted midwives in Tennessee, she became well-regarded and sought-after for working deftly and gently even without her left hand.

Howling, the woman awakened distant wolves calling from the shadows.

When she finally quieted, the woman stared at Willa, her wild eyes framed by drenched hair, slick with sweat like lacquer.

Willa imagined what the woman saw and knew she was a sight, her tattered dress bloodstained and rotting, her body hungry and unbathed, her left wrist ending in a stump, an old amputation from childhood. Despite her wounds, she was still strong, her skin burnished from the sun, muscles toned from laboring in tobacco fields, when not helping expectant mothers.

"You think I'm ruined? We can't let anyone know," the woman whispered.

Willa shuddered, remembering how she had attempted to ruin her value by chopping off her left hand. Cruel as he sometimes was, Jon Turner kept her from traders who wanted to torture her to death, perhaps assuming no one would want her after she butchered her own body. She chopped her left hand clean off the wrist in front of the auctioneer and bidders while hoping it would make her worthless to them. She was finished being a victim. At Mason's insistence, Jon bought her, offering a high price, though her left hand was lying at her feet in a pool of fresh blood on the auctioneer's stage, where she was bleeding to death. She held her severed hand up for all to see, daring them to want to possess her. The auctioneer sold her fast. Mason had surgical training and gave her whiskey as he rushed her away to cauterize and stitch her wound, closing her wrist with a flap of skin. She healed better and more quickly than expected and began to apprentice to the elderly midwife on the plantation, learning all the secrets from the old woman. Eventually becoming the new midwife, Willa was astounded that so many captive women on the plantation gave birth to pale children, so many of them twins. Twins ran in the Turner family for many generations.

Now, in Concord woods, Willa prepared to midwife yet another woman. This woman was free, though alone. Willa could tell by the look in her eyes.

"How far, how long?" Willa whispered.

"Two months, maybe three," said the woman, doubling over.

Willa held the woman's hand, to guide her through the pain, and thought of Viv.

Willa would always suspect it was Mason who convinced Henry Ward Beecher to send Viv to take photographs of the Turners' infamous enslaved gentlemen and ladies. The first photographer, a northerner who had once photographed Lincoln, didn't get far, but when Viv Hayden arrived and Mason introduced her as his fiancé, old Jon Turner was charmed by her freckles, fiery red hair, and jade eyes. Those freckles! Willa could see them, even now, how they stood out on Viv's pale skin, like dead leaves scattered over snow.

When Viv said her passion was photography, Jon ordered two custom-made cameras just for her, as a wedding gift. Jon never guessed Viv's true passion—Godfrey—until it was too late. Viv asked to photograph Willa and Godfrey and all the Turner family and all its captives. Long rumored in the North, enslaved ladies were true to life in the Turner plantation, where appearances weren't always reality, since a captive's status was based on the condition of his or her mother. As in nature, the mother was the one who bore deepest burden, her life bought in blood.

"Help me, please!" The woman screamed.

Willa put her bloodstained shawl over the woman's mouth. She couldn't forget what had happened at the plantation, as no one could have believed it without seeing with his own eyes. She knew why Mason couldn't live with it, why Beecher wanted to get involved. Even Confederates who hadn't wanted to abolish slavery thought differently after seeing the photographs Viv Turner had taken. In those portraits, features of enslaved women, children, and men mirrored the family features of slaveholders. They were all Turners—so many of them twins—and all the Turners having light skin, warm and bright veiled almond eyes, strong noses, high cheek bones, those chiseled features like classical statues.

"Hush, hush, now."

The woman vomited on fallen leaves. An owl called, as if lonely for a mate.

Willa had seen women bleeding. Many, themselves almost children, became Clara Turner's obsession. Clara, Jon's sister, never married but managed the household activities of the plantation. There were rumors that as a child she had no dolls since she treated the captive children as her dolls and, as she became an adult, she still saw the children as playthings. Any captive woman expecting at the Turner plantation had to be locked up and tied down. The Turners fetched a higher price at auction, due to their pale complexions, though Jon rarely sold them, since Clara wouldn't allow him. Jon did purchase more women from time to time. Willa had been bought at auction at thirteen because Mason couldn't stand to watch her die.

Who was worse—Jon or his sister, Clara? Both were one half of sets of identical twins, separated in childhood; the other half, a boy named Henry Turner and a girl named Ruby Turner, had been taken away from the plantation by their mother after an infamous separation, when Ruby and Henry and their mother moved to Concord, leaving the plantation forever. But that was long, long ago, long before Willa was brought to the Turner plantation, so all she knew of the past were rumors. And yet these rumors were why she had come to Concord. She knew Mason would go to the other half of his family, the Northerners, and that Godfrey would likely try to follow him.

As the woman wept, Willa calculated the distance to Ruby Turner's boardinghouse. Mason had drawn a crude map for her and for Godfrey but Willa didn't know if she had the courage to face Ruby Turner. Ruby was rumored to be a free-thinking woman, unlike her twin. She was supposedly supportive of the rights of women, an abolitionist well before the war ended slavery. But she looked like Clara, the torturer, the veiled witch of Tennessee.

Clara was just the opposite of Ruby, or so Mason said. He said Clara was dead now, murdered, but Willa was never sure because Clara was rumored to have died many times in the past. The old people remembered Clara first became touched in the head when Ruby was taken away in childhood.

"I've seen this hundreds of times before," Willa whispered to the woman. It was beautiful, brutal, nasty business. If this woman was free from what haunted Willa, what was she doing alone in the woods?

The woman cried out, again. The sharp sudden cry shattered the tranquility of the misty wood. Willa stroked the woman's shoulders, and the woman began weeping softly, whispering, "Can't you slow it down?"

Of course, Willa couldn't help helping, though she was still searching for Godfrey. She loved Godfrey more than anyone, including herself, though she once thought she would never love any man. Now they were both free, they were planning to marry, once they both reached Concord but he was nowhere in sight. She didn't even know if he was still alive. They had been separated in Tennessee because of Viv, who was foolish enough to fall in love with him and to show it, unlike so many other Little Anns who admired him secretly.

Willa never knew if Godfrey was Black or white. Godfrey had been Mason's age, like a brother to him, even rumored to be his twin. The two had grown up as brothers until Clara forbade them to play together because she caught Godfrey reading to Mason in the library.

The woman's hand wilted like a lily sweating droplets of rain. She was losing the child.

Listening to the howl of wolves, Willa built a fire to keep animals away, not wanting the blood on the ground to attract predators or scavengers. Coyotes, wolves, and farm dogs howled as the woman screamed and bled. "Shhhhhh, shhhhhhhhhhh," Willa said. Wild dogs, once tame, were the most dangerous. Having lost their natural fear of man, they had no respect for woman.

"What's your name?" Willa asked the young woman.

"Hattie," she said. "Hattie Grove."

It was like every other time before—in helping this woman, Willa became so close to her, closer than she had planned or wanted.

Soon they were like sisters by a pact sealed in blood. Blood on dresses, blood on the ground, blood on Hattie's hands, and on Willa's right hand, her only hand. Blood on their faces, their hair. When the worst was over, Willa wrapped what was left in rags. Willa cradled it, offering it to river, washing blood away with sorrow.

Hattie was weeping, now in relief.

"What shall I do?" Hattie asked.

"Just rest if you can."

"I didn't mean for this to happen."

Willa wondered if some women do. Willa was barren and, at the plantation, this was the greatest blessing. Now free, she felt sad to think what was and wasn't possible.

Hattie drifted to sleep beside the fire, her head resting on Willa's lap.

After an hour, Willa woke Hattie, knowing she would need to shield her.

Willa lit a torch and led Hattie back through the woods to the clearing.

They stared at each other and Willa knew they were saying goodbye.

"Your hand," Hattie whispered.

Willa merely shook her head. "Follow me," she said, taking Hattie down a path through scrub trees toward the farm road, where a man in a faded uniform, a Union man, stacked crates for a bonfire near the apple orchards.

"It's All Hallows' Eve," said Hattie.

"What?" Willa asked, worried there might be other folks as superstitious and demented as Clara Turner.

"Willa," said Hattie. "I need to be careful not to be seen, especially by him. Before the war, that man and I used to belong to each other."

Willa shuddered. Any talk of one person owning another felt wrong. How many men still attempted to own their women?

"Right," said Willa.

"Hide me," said Hattie.

Behind a large oak, Willa stood with Hattie, waiting for the man to turn away.

"Who is he, anyway?" Willa asked, realizing the man was also missing a hand, his left hand, same as hers.

"Sampson Redlaw, Major General," said Hattie, shivering in her bloody dress. "We were engaged to be married, before the war."

"It's his child you lost?" Immediately, Willa was sorry. The question felt wrong, as if a child was a thing for a woman to lose, an object to be misplaced or discarded.

"Another man's, his friend."

"Hattie?"

"He can't see us?"

Hiding in shadow, they held each. Behind the oak, shivering. Hattie leaned on Willa.

Willa felt kinship with Hattie, something like sisterhood, but didn't trust the feeling. She had been betrayed before. She remembered Godfrey, how he and Mason Turner were once like brothers, both the same age, with the same father. Some whispered they had the same mother, but how could that be true? The woman who had nursed them both as infants, the one who looked after all the children and nursed them, began setting secret meals for Godfrey and Mason in the library. They ate together for years, growing up that way, brothers, half-brothers, because Jon Turner lay with most of his women, calling them out into the field, never acknowledging those women's children as his own, so he would never have to acknowledged his father had done the same, that his women were his father's daughters, his sisters. Even though he never spoke of it, he must have known why they looked like him and Clara and Mason, why their skin was so light they could have passed for white. And some did, getting away, disappearing into northern cities.

The captive male with the lightest skin was Godfrey. When Godfrey and Mason grew up together in the big house, some of the old folks said both of their mothers had been pregnant at the same time. But no one knew for certain. Some said Mason's mother died during the birth, hidden away in the back rooms of the mansion after a priest was rumored to have performed wedding vows with last rites. Since no one knew who she was or who Godfrey's mother was, there were also whispers that Mason and Godfrey's mother was the same enslaved woman and that they were twins born to her, together, one being white and the other Black. One twin was deemed free while the other was deemed a possession.

Godfrey and Mason were older than Willa—five years older than she. When she arrived at the plantation at age thirteen, her left wrist still bleeding, she had to trust the stories she heard from the old midwife. Because the midwife's skin was dark like Willa's, bluish black like Concord grapes, the rest of the captive people, especially the women, appeared very pale by contrast.

Most of the women were in love with Godfrey, like Willa was. Willa lived and breathed for the aged midwife's stories, since the midwife was the one who raised Godfrey like a mother, knowing his secrets, helping Willa to capture his heart. There were lots of stories about Godfrey and Mason, rumors in the old Turner mansion. Stories to fill the night until in crept the light of dawn.

Concord woods filled with mist in dappled sunlight fading, the air crisp with the scent of fresh fallen leaves crushed under foot.

Hattie was still bleeding, profusely. This worried Willa, who wanted to see Hattie safe without leading anyone back to her own hiding place.

Blood, coppery, misted the air that Halloween evening as the wolves howled, again, calling to each other.

3.

Henry Turner heard laughter in the evening. A couple ran past him on the worn trail. They were wearing bone masks and racing toward the woods, as if they expected someone to chase them. Apparently, the Halloween mischief had begun.

Henry waved at farmers preparing the bonfire in Turner's Field. They stacked crates and old boards and broken furniture. Henry approached the women's boardinghouse run by his sister, Ruby. Expansive with four levels (basement, main floor, second story, and attic), its design emphasized the best of both worlds, Grecian columns and Gothic arches—the perfect house for a Halloween party.

Ruby's Halloween parties were legendary throughout all of Concord.

The housemaid, Kora, welcomed Henry inside the boardinghouse. The great room cloistered scents of kerosene, soot, and tallow in oil lamps burning lard.

Guests gathered around the parlor piano for a sing. Henry listened as he stood by the hearth fire. Manipulating the bellows to blow up the flames, he sped the kindling in time to music.

Ruby approached the crackling flame and smiled at Henry. He smiled back in secret sadness. He and Ruby had just lost their other halves, their identical twins, Jon and Clara. Perhaps that was why after all these long decades far into middle age, he had suddenly fallen in love. Henry wanted to tell Ruby that he would be bringing uninvited guests to her Halloween party. Because it was a dinner party, he knew Ruby would not appreciate surprise guests.

* * *

Henry had met the twin girls, Spiritualist mediums, at Town Hall during the costume contest and couldn't help but invite them. Maggie and Valerie were identical twins, like Clara and Ruby, like Jon and Henry. Valerie, the twin in a wheelchair, captured Henry's heart.

Maggie said to Henry, "Sir, you look just like a man we knew in Tennessee."

Henry knew Maggie meant Jon and was delighted the twins were acquainted with his deceased brother until he began to realize they had lived as Jon's captives.

"I'm so sorry," he had apologized to the twins profusely while feeling such shame to realize they had been imprisoned by a member of his family, his own twin brother, Jon Turner, a slaveholder and plantation owner in Tennessee. "You must see a monster when you look at me?" asked Henry, knowing they had a right to loathe him.

"No," said Maggie, speaking for herself and her sister, as was her habit. "We see something different than you imagine. Besides, we didn't spend much time with Jon. Clara was the one we spent much time with since we were children."

"Clara?" asked Henry.

Maggie explained that Clara, Henry's estranged sister, had taught the twins how to be mediums and how communicate with the dead through séance and materialization.

Trying to remember Clara but only able to see Ruby's face, Henry stared down at the silent sister, Valerie, who sat so stiffly and properly in her wheelchair with her face elegantly veiled. He thought of what Jon had done and he despised his family for being former slaveholders but not as much as he despised himself as he beheld the slender girl in her wheelchair. He knew it was improper to dream of loving Valerie. Yet it was all he could imagine. He invited both twins to Ruby's dumb supper and wondered if they would come.

Now, not knowing how to tell Ruby what he was thinking, Henry merely told her he was looking forward to the dumb supper. Ruby's parties were much beloved and attended by Henry's friends, returning soldiers, foremost among them a hearty ginger-haired amputee, Major General Sampson Redlaw, who was missing his left hand, amputated at the wrist.

Visitors and boarders conversed beside the parlor fire in Ruby's boardinghouse. Kora served a lovely black tea scented with rose petals from Ruby's greenhouse. Ruby introduced Henry to Mason Turner, his nephew he had never met, formerly of Tennessee.

"A true Southern gentleman," Ruby whispered, embarrassed.

"Whoever degrades another degrades me, and whatever is done or said returns at last to me, and whatever I do or say I also return," said Henry, quoting poetry because Mason appeared to be a man born into wealth, accustomed to the good life, likely not even realizing how wrong it was that others labored without rights for generations to provide for his lifestyle. Just like his father, Jon.

"I'm a former slaveholder," Mason said. "I'm not proud of my inheritance or what my family has done."

"You mean our family?" whispered Ruby.

"You fought for the Confederates?" asked Henry, sipping his tea in restrained outrage, though he knew his outrage was hypocritical since he had been born down South in the same plantation as Mason and was also a child of slaveholders, until his mother changed all that. His mother, god rest her soul, broke away from the plantation, taking Henry and Ruby with her to leave the shameful life behind.

"When captured by the Union, my medical knowledge allowed me to assist Dr. Ian Burrows, who tended to the wounded," Mason said.

"Ah," said Henry, who knew the brave doctor.

After Mason left the room, Ruby whispered to Henry, "Mason and Viv want to keep their marriage a secret, to act as if it never happened, but won't say why."

Henry stared at Viv, one of Ruby's new boarders warming herself by the fire, sitting catlike on hearthstones, her silken red curls falling out of black velvet ribbon. Viv nervously touched her nose and cheeks, brushing her fingertips over her freckles. Henry wondered why she seemed so nervous, then realized she was hiding something.

In love with a freedwoman young enough to be his granddaughter, Henry had his own secrets and schemes, enough to respect Viv's. Intrigued by the silent Valerie, he now wondered why she sat veiled in her wheelchair, never speaking but only communicating through Maggie. Never had he met such delicate, alluring young women. Maggie, Valerie's speaker, never said much of that other life before the war when Valerie could walk and talk. Henry realized something awful had happened because they had not been free. His feelings for the twins made him envision an ally in Viv. He was also a great fan of Reverend Henry Ward Beecher's sermons. His devotion to Rev. Beecher was what first drew him to Viv, who claimed to know Beecher.

"What has driven them apart?" whispered Henry, smiling so Viv wouldn't guess what he was saying.

Since leaving a husband could ruin a woman's reputation, Henry knew why Ruby agreed to keep Viv's failed marriage a secret, in hopes of creating a better union for her with a good man who might not judge her. Mason did not require the spectacle of separation, or so Ruby said.

Henry worried for Ruby. Having no child or husband, Ruby was vulnerable, or so he thought. He remembered the questionable dealings of Ruby's identical twin, his sister, Clara Turner, who had been like a mother to Mason on the plantation. According to Ruby, Clara raised Mason, taking the place of his mother, after his mother died giving birth to him. Henry considered Ruby too trusting, too willing to get involved in the problems of acquaintances, strangers, and family—especially with a family like theirs.

"I never understood our family," whispered Ruby, as if she, too, were thinking of the old plantation.

Henry was concerned since Ruby's childhood friend, Lara Hayden, had perished in a Boston apartment fire, supposedly along with Ruby's long estranged twin, their sister, Clara Turner. Clara had become a medium embraced by Boston's Spiritualist community after she left the plantation following Jon's death. Neighbors had warned Henry that Ruby might be in danger by having a dumb supper in her boardinghouse because Clara had been seen so many times after she supposedly died.

Three different times, Clara was reported to have died by fire. First, decades ago in Tennessee when she was a teenager, then when she was a mature woman during a Civil-War plantation fire, and finally in the apartment fire in Boston. In that most recent fire, Lara and Samuel Hayden were said to have burned together with Clara during a séance. If authorities and investigators were to be believed, the fire that killed Samuel, Lara, and Clara was an accident, a common enough occurrence in row houses heated by chimneys and lit by gas lamps and tallow. The fire had burned so hot that only very few bones were found, not enough for even a full skeleton. It was unclear if only one body was in the ash or many bodies with missing or consumed bones. A story told by bones. Nothing proven. No motive. No murderer ever found. Perhaps it was all a freakish accident?

Viv, Lara Hayden's daughter, seemed strange—secretive, nervous, almost as if she were putting on a performance. But why?

Perhaps Viv was the missing link. She was just the type easily influenced by the likes of Clara Turner and Beecher, the two of them enemies, who might have used Viv for separate, competing purposes. It frightened Henry every time he heard townspeople describe his estranged sister: "Clara looks just like Ruby in a wig and girdle but with angry eyes."

Henry approached Viv, slyly. He sensed she wanted to tell him something but perhaps didn't know how.

Each time Henry spoke to Viv, he felt Viv possessed such fevered Southern eloquence for a Northern woman. Perhaps unaware of the extent of Viv's duplicity, Ruby displayed the Hayden sisters like rare hothouse flowers from her glass-walled garden. Viv perfected a tantalizing pantomime of flirtation, a delicate dance like spiders mating. Sometimes she used only her eyes to control men, who seemed entranced by her. But was she really as self-possessed as she now seemed?

Henry winced, remembering the story of her screams—a story told to him by rumor of the plantation fire. It was the fire that killed Jon after he had botched a lynching started to protect Viv's honor. Henry had heard rumors that Viv howled on the old plantation while searching for her lover, the fabled Godfrey, an enslaved man doomed to die by hanging after being caught with her. They said Godfrey disappeared somehow and started the fire. Some people didn't believe that. Some whispered it was a lie, that there was no Godfrey and that Jon Turner set his own house ablaze to burn Viv and his sister Clara, but Viv escaped.

Now that Mason Turner had arrived in Concord, along with Viv, Henry wanted to approach Mason, again, to ask him about Jon and Godfrey, to see if Godfrey was real. Henry was trying to decide how best to approach the delicate topic. Mason had lost his home and his father. The death of Jon and the burning of the plantation were real. But was the legend of Godfrey?

"Tell me about Godfrey," Henry whispered.

"Godfrey," Viv whispered, holding her belly as if someone had struck her. "Sweet Godfrey."

Henry stared out the window while wondering if Viv's Godfrey could be the same murderous hero in tales whispered before hearth fires.

Outside the window, Sampson Redlaw piled scrap wood for the bonfire. Henry watched him. In the field near the orchard, mules roamed. An expert at animal husbandry, Redlaw tended to mules with gentle authority. Henry sighed, finding Redlaw even more admirable now he was wounded. He wondered why wounded men, especially soldiers and amputees, filled him with longing.

"What is it?" Viv asked.

Henry stole one last long glance out the window, knowing well what Sampson and Ruby were preparing. Every All Hallows' Eve, Ruby, acting as matchmaker, threw an annual Halloween party with a great bonfire to burn a witch effigy, offering free hayrides to unmarried gentlemen and ladies who dressed in costume before attending her dumb supper. This Halloween, unmarried soldiers in uniform were honored guests.

4.

"Attending my dumb supper tonight, Mr. Redlaw?" Ruby Turner asked Sampson Redlaw on Halloween evening, when he was working outdoors on his little farm, which housed mules for sale and rent. "Now is almost time for the hayride."

Sampson Redlaw nodded, realizing he had forgotten to send his reply.

"Why is it called a dumb supper?" a petite young woman asked.

Sampson tried to remember her name and thought it was Belle.

"Because you must eat in complete silence, as Mr. Redlaw knows," said Ruby.

"But why?" A homely woman with a goat face asked.

Sampson felt the petite girl staring at his injury.

"People have always sensed the spirits," said Ruby. "Think of shadow people, dreams of premonition, soft whispers, ghostly wind on your hair, your eyes playing tricks on you, ears hearing voices when no one else is there. Every time you've gone somewhere for the first time and felt you had been there before? That's ghostly communion, otherworldly communication."

Ruby's keen indigo eyes contrasted starkly with her unruly silver curls. Near the mule gate, her gaggle of ladies winked away flies. Ruby explained, again, her boarders were the Hayden sisters: Aria, Grace, Belle, and Viv.

Sampson was surprised to find the sisters so diverse in manner and style.

The freckled sister was Viv.

The petite sister staring at his amputation was Belle.

Aria was the unattractive sister.

Sampson fancied the tall, regal, and steely-eyed sister, Grace.

"Grace," Sampson repeated without thinking. Next to all the others, her reserve impressed him. She never once stared at his amputation. She radiated refined sophistication, a true lady in the way she held herself, her back so straight, her gloved hands clasped neatly in front of her. Aria was homely. Belle was childish. Viv seemed haunted, even with her curvy figure and girlish freckles. Grace, though, was full of dignity, as if knowing her worth. A pity he had accidentally offended her on the boardinghouse road by colliding with her in the dark near the well. He had been too nervous to apologize.

The women laughed and Sampson was dumbfounded. He could find no excuse to talk to Grace and was glad that the dumb supper meant no talking. Even the combs in Grace's hair befuddled him. She gazed at him coldly. A single strand fell out of her combs. She reached to straighten it. He noticed her lovely hands, fine and strong, her arms willowy in the sleeves of her mourning dress. Though she was dressed all in black, she wore a hummingbird broach with matching earbobs. She smirked. He raised an eyebrow.

"Sampson?" asked Ruby. "Is everything all right? Maybe you should take a break, and let some other man tend to these mules?"

"No," he said.

Ruby turned her attention back to the women, her charges. Concord's most trusted matchmaker, she guided youngish virgins, fallen women, and desperate spinsters to respectable marriages with eligible men. Decades ago, when her hair was redder than his, Redlaw fantasized about holding her brilliant head in his hands. She was his mother's age and he had been pursuing her since he was a child. The fact that he was a war hero meant nothing now because gazing at her made him feel like a child again.

When he was just sixteen, Henry caught him in Ruby's boardinghouse, spying on her. Thank god, Ruby and Henry recognized the curious boy he was. Misguided but harmless, Sampson had hidden in the boardinghouse often, to spy on Ruby and the women, who made a game of searching for him when he was a child.

Knowing that women who boarded with Miss Turner sought her advice on men and matchmaking, Sampson was keenly aware he was now one of Concord's most eligible bachelors, but he was also concerned that women would regard him differently because he was not a whole man.

Though Ruby Turner remained as enigmatic as Henry, also an expert on love and long unmarried, Sampson hoped to learn more of what Ruby was planning.

"Ask questions in silence and the spirits will answer," whispered Ruby.

"Why," asked Viv, "will the dead speak? Will the invisible guest eat?"

"Food has been offered to the dead throughout history, from prehistoric man to the Celts to the Egyptians, Romans, Mexicans, Chinese, Japanese, and even the Roman Catholic Church," said Ruby.

"How will we know the invisible guest is with us?" asked Grace. "Would he ever need to sit down? If he has no body to rest, why sit?"

"What makes you think the invisible guest will be a he?" asked Sampson.

"Tonight, you must gaze into mirrors in darkness," said Ruby. "A face will appear. Now, Mr. Redlaw has readied the wagons, so fetch your masks. Before it gets too dark to see your costumes!"

Sampson laughed. Harnessing his mules, he stole a glance at tightly corseted mourning dresses.

"Mr. Redlaw," said Ruby, "behave, especially tonight. You never know what might happen."

He grinned hoping Miss Turner wouldn't notice how hopeful he was beneath his mask of dirt and tangled hair.

Struggling to deal with the effects of amputation and what that would mean in marriage, he attempted to focus on the night's festivities. All during the hayrides, women would be listening for spirits, and anticipating the dumb supper, where a dead man, woman, or child was promised to attend as an invisible guest.

Even if it was just a game, the dumb supper changed the way everyone ate because there had to be perfect silence. Of course, there were rules but Sampson thought it foolish to save an empty chair for the dead because there was already a place reserved in each of their hearts.

5.

Earlier in the day, Viv had framed the glossy cotton paper, already dipped in silver nitrate and dried beneath the glass negatives of the couple in the bone masks. Securing the glass and the paper, she had printed with sunlight. As the image darkened, the couple emerged in terrifying glory.

Viv longed to ask Miss Turner and Kora who the bone-mask couple were and why they had come to her, pretending to be the prize winners. Touching her freckles lightly, Viv wondered if it was an elaborate prank or a misunderstanding. Or, maybe someone was trying to scare her? If so, they succeeded.

And yet, no damage was done. Her cameras were safe. She still couldn't believe she was lucky enough to have been able to keep the cameras, in spite of what had happened.

The cameras were gifts from her father-in-law, Jon Tuner. She guarded them closely, having rescued the cameras, her photographs, and photography equipment from the fire at Twin Oaks by hiding it all in the chapel. Shortly before the plantation became unstable and the mansion burned, she paid a great deal for a carrier to deliver her cameras, equipment, and photograph books by carriage to Boston, for safe keeping. Later, after fleeing the South, she reclaimed them, taking them from Boston to Concord and to her room in Miss Ruby's boardinghouse.

Working with her wet-plate camera when she lived the life of a Southern belle, she often spent her days at the Turner plantation with silver nitrate. She was a rare woman, trusted with poisons.

She mixed her own chemicals and prepared her own wet-plate negatives. The negatives had to be prepared, exposed, and developed within minutes, before the emulsion dried. Then as now, she used her closet as a darkroom, her exquisite gowns without a home.

Producing photographs from wet plates involved many steps. She coated a clean sheet of glass evenly with collodion. In her darkroom, she immersed the coated plate in a silver nitrate solution, sensitizing it to light. After it was sensitized, the wet negative was placed in a light-tight holder and inserted into her camera, which already had been positioned and focused. The "dark slide" protected the negative from light. The lens cap was removed for several seconds, allowing light to expose the plate. And then, the "dark slide" was inserted back into the plate holder, which was then removed from the camera.

In her darkroom, she had already removed the last glass-plate negative from the plate holder and developed it, washed it in water, and fixed it so that the image would not fade, then washed it again and dried it before coating the negative with a varnish to protect the surface.

One by one, when correctly exposed to light, the images "printed" and settled strikingly clear and crisp. She loved the surprise of watching images develop. It was like magic the way the light worked on the paper. It was a pleasure to fix, set, tone, and frame new photographs. She liked to group photographs to compare them to each other, since they always seemed to tell a story. First, the terrifying couple in their wigs and bone masks, so mysterious. Second, the sweet young couple, the cat and mouse, so trusting. The images were in stark contrast, one of horror and menace and the other of tenderness and love. And yet, both images had something in common—the sense of union.

Viv printed additional photographs on paper for her own collection and mounted them in books. In the past, working for abolitionists undercover while living at the Turner plantation in Tennessee, she would send her photographs to Rev. Beecher. She was still taking photographs for him, as she had all these years. Now, Beecher had tasked her with photographing Ruby's secret room, but this meant finding ways to sneak and lug a camera into Grace's room and through the hidden door in Grace's closet. Beecher had told her about the room and she wanted to capture it for history, but the one time she tried, there were odd images that showed up on the photographs of the room—images that shouldn't be there. There were shadow children, though she saw no children in the room. There were also shadow women, though the women weren't there. She thought there was something wrong with her camera, until Beecher warned her that he would tell his church what he suspected Viv had captured—ghosts in the photographs.

Beecher often asked her, by letter, if the rumors about Godfrey were true, if her virtue were compromised, if Mason was good to her, and if the marriage had been a success. She lied to keep his unholy interest away from her.

She was good with men and good with poisons and good with cameras but never good with guiding her own heart.

Because of the chemicals used in the photography process, she was familiar with ethyl ether, acetic, and sulfuric acid, which had to be mixed by hand.

Her life seemed a series of fragile glass plates made valuable by skill and poison.

Long ago, she had become inspired and obsessed with creating sophisticated three-dimensional images or "stereoviews" for displaying life-like images of the Turner plantation. Now those images were all that were left of the plantation, which had burnt for days during the final moments of the war.

She had used a twin-lens camera to capture the same image (the mansion burning) from two separate lenses, in much the same way that two human eyes capture the same image from slightly different angles on the head. The images were developed using the same wet-plate process, producing two of the same image on one plate glass.

Once processed, Viv would place the two stereo images onto a single viewing card—the stereograph. These stereoview cards could be inserted into viewers creating a 3D image. Alone in her room, she often stared into her stereoscope. Gazing at stereoview photographs of the people of the old planation was like holding a vanished world in her hands. Devouring a vanished land with her eyes, she saw Godfrey.

6.

Moonlit alfalfa fields spread like green velvet blankets surrounding orchards and stables where jack-o'-lanterns glowed. Flames lured the last looper moths of the season, shedding golden light on mourning dresses. Hundreds of pale insects with flame-lit wings fluttered like snow in wind. Near the bonfires, women with gloved hands batted looper moths.

As caterpillars, these clever insects tended to move along grasses in a looping gate, hiding from their enemies by day, feeding by night.

In times of war, certain men and women survived by moving like the looper-moth caterpillars, feeding in the dark, traveling to conceal themselves from others, even when they were right beside them, hiding in the same grasses, the same woods, the same buildings. It was terrifying to think people might move like that, again, to hide from each other in close proximity, now that the war was over.

Sampson Redlaw thought the looper-moth caterpillars were like soldiers who had recently hidden in fields with him, under his command in meadows, parks, along roadsides, near farmhouses burning, after they had set them ablaze. The moths, active until late autumn, seemed to be gathering in a final celebration on the fields with the partygoers this evening. Ordinary looking, light brown, even ugly during the day, at night near the bonfires, the moths appeared illuminated, breathtaking, wings capturing light.

Soldiers basked in the amber glow of bonfires. With amputations, prosthetics, and battle scars, these uniformed men approached women with veiled eyes, costumes obscuring downcast faces as snow-like wings fluttered around their heads.

Firelight caught in ebony jewels' glittering. Luminous

jewelry lured moths to bejeweled women, and Sampson felt grateful for his mask of leaves.

"Plague take it," he said.

Trying to ignore eyelike jewels winking over women's bosoms near the fire, he warned Sergeant Jerry Rickett about Miss Belle Hayden's monstrous mourning dress. Velvet stroked and swallowed Belle's short legs in a sensuous manner. Her tiny waist synched tight, a girdle constricted her bosom, causing her white breasts to float on black lace like two prized peaches shelved on prominent display.

Redlaw mistrusted women who had been without men too long. War had a way of making ordinary men heroes in the eyes of women.

Across the twilight field, the stiff dress imprisoned Belle's body as she grinned at Sampson. At some angles, her dress was like a giant black cat, at other angles, like an enormous black parasite eating her alive. If her body was a host to her costume, Sampson thought many fashionable ladies were elegantly devoured by clothing.

Twelve candles were a lot to jump over. It was nearly impossible in a long, full, heavy skirted dress of black velvet, intricate black-thread embroidery. The cage, far too large for Miss Belle, accentuated its architectural framework of fancy crinoline shaped like a lampshade. Trimmed in exotic rows of ebony ribbon shadowing scallops, the dress was a fire hazard.

Belle hollered, running on short legs. The dress fought her all the way, the cage swinging back and forth. Her sisters howled, and looper moths scattered. Belle skipped past candles, past wagons and horses, past jack-o'-lanterns in neat rows, far down the darkening field. Moonlight illuminated her silhouette, covered in glowing moths. Her shadow came running back to candles. Sampson knew she would never make it. Leaping diminutively, she landed on the sixth candle, extinguishing it with a petite shoe before falling on the remaining candles, catching her dress afire.

"Damn it," Sampson whispered as her sisters screamed,

watching Belle burn.

She made the mistake of racing away, as if she could outrun the flames.

"Stop!" Sampson called.

In her panic, Belle stirred the wind.

Sampson leapt through the air, tackling her, so she was pinned beneath his good arm. Shielding his amputation as she fought, he covered her with his body. Over six-foot tall, he was much larger than she, struggling, panicking, fighting him. He tried to extinguish her by rolling in dirt, leaves, rotting apples. Finally, he had the fire out, though she was weeping, her dark eyes sparkling, collecting tears. He picked her up, cradled her like a frightened child. He was good with children, once having been the eldest of six brothers. They were all now lost to war.

"There, there," he whispered, wiping away her tears with his long ginger hair. He never carried a handkerchief, something his mother once scolded him for. "Alright," he said, setting Belle gently on the dirt, her skirt now burnt away. As he removed his coat, she pointed to her tiny toes, petite pale legs exposed in singed pantaloons, raw in the dress's cage, shoes singed.

Covering her with his long coat, "This will keep you warm," he whispered.

"You saved me."

He grinned.

She jumped up, wrapping her arms around his neck, swinging from him as if he were a tree, hugging as if she didn't want to let go.

Christ, he thought.

When he sat her back on her feet, she gazed up at him.

Hay-filled wagons approached.

Chris Datchery relit all twelve candles, then hollered, "Sampson, show us how it's done?"

The masked crowd cheered and gathered round the candles in a wide arc, silhouetted by bonfires.

Sampson considered his wound: left wrist, throbbing,

crusted bandages covering the amputation. He had ranked first among the candle jumpers of his youth. Everyone was chanting his name.

Sampson ran far down the dark field through the orchard. The partygoers must have thought he had run away, the bonfire and the silhouettes tiny in the distance. Taking a breath, he raced back on his long legs. Hollering, he leapt high, clearing all the little flames. He didn't put out a single candle, and the party guests roared.

"That's how it's done," Jerry Rickett said. "Sampson Redlaw, master candle jumper! Nothing ever keeps a good man down. Not even the old saw bones."

Dr. Burrows approached, and Jerry mumbled a quick apology.

"At least he's still alive," the doctor said.

Unlike many former soldiers who still blamed the doctor for hacking off their limbs, Sampson felt no blame, though it took three surgeries to finish the job and the wound was still festering.

"Hello, Doctor," Sampson said, smiling down into Ian Burrows's kind eyes. Burrows was a small man with a big heart, and the choices he had to make were not easy. Hard choices were how he saved so many lives.

"Good to see you, my friend," said Dr. Burrows, stepping onto the wagon filled with fresh hay gleaming in moonlight. Always the ladies' man, despite his ongoing dealings with hysteria, the doctor assisted several women onto the wagon.

Aged forty-eight, the doctor had served as a field surgeon for the Union during the war. His large steady hands were complimented by a cool head under pressure. He was deaf in his left ear from the sound of cannon fire. He often smoked a pipe and held his liquor well, despite his short stature. A skillful fisherman, Dr. Burrows had enormous veiny forearms and keen bloodshot eyes.

"See you at the dumb supper, friend," said Sampson.

Dr. Burrows waved.

The doctor's wagon soon filled, but one woman lingered, standing back. Belle Hayden. With a sinking in his gullet, Sampson realized she was waiting for him. Her marvelously austere sister, Grace Hayden, had not waited. A tall person, like Sampson, Grace had already boarded the first wagon near the doctor. Sampson regretted there was no place for him in that wagon, the one with strong, young, slender horses driven by Chris Datchery.

"Take care, Sampson," Chris called, lashing the horses with a firm and yet gentle stoke.

As Henry Turner's hired man, Chris earned a living by serving as a human guard dog. Thick Irish accent, broken teeth, nose slightly crooked from past breaks, Chris had big knuckles from fighting and cut an imposing figure, his ears misshapen, scars on his eyes and lips. He hid his infamous cauliflower ears under his dark curls. Stitches puckered his left eyebrow, a crescent-shaped scar near the eye pulled tightly, squinting unevenly whenever he laughed.

Chris and Sampson were friends, but what Chris didn't know could have destroyed them. Long before Sampson was engaged to Hattie, he had been visiting an older Irish fancy woman in Boston. She sang him lullabies and Sampson felt she treated him differently than other clients. They began writing letters during the war. In these letters, she confessed her son, a former professional boxer, was serving in the military. Sampson sought Chris out, convincing him to join his regiment and to move to Concord after the war, even getting Chris a job working for Henry Turner, never telling him why.

Chris was like a son to Sampson, even though there was less than ten years' difference in their ages. Because Sampson had lost his brothers, Chris was dear to him. He had promised Chris's mother, Rose Datchery, never to reveal the truth that she was dying of syphilis. Rose had abruptly stopped answering his letters. When Sampson last visited Boston, she was gone.

"Hello, friend," Henry Turner called while waving to Sampson. Henry waddled beside a handsome wagon loading soldiers in uniform. Old Henry Turner, as wealthy as he was plump, owned several sets of horses and wagons, but Henry wasn't a gifted wagoner like his hired man, the wiry Chris Datchery. Henry, who could only control fat horses, often claimed to have avoided matrimony because he didn't want a woman telling him what to do. Large with a round belly, he huffed air when he walked and often did not leave his house for days. He was rarely lonely, since he hosted gambling parties and the occasional séance.

Having a bout of rheumatic fever as a young boy, Henry suffered a weak heart ever since, so Sampson guessed Henry was a virgin, like Ruby. Henry, who never fought in the war because he bought a substitute, seemed no threat to anyone, even the invalid girl he had met at the costume contest and strangely adored. The girl had recently arrived to Concord with her twin, and Sampson had yet to lay eyes on her, assuming the twins shy. Sampson started for a moment, wondering why the twins weren't among the guests at the hayride.

"Mr. Redlaw," Belle said, approaching Sampson. "Major General, shall we ride together?"

"Why not."

Dark eyes flinty, she stared down at her burnt shoes, her lithe tongue flicking over her pearly little teeth. Sampson studied the paleness of her porcelain skin, lovely in a doll-like fashion. He helped her onto the wagon. She clung to his right arm, nestling into fresh hay, his coat wrapped over her legs like a blanket.

Jerry Rickett, Hattie Grove, and Nick Dalton joined them in the wagon along with Dr. Burrows's assistant, Mason Turner, who was also Ruby's nephew and a former Confederate soldier who once had been captured and forced to care for wounded Union soldiers in the hospital camps. Sampson and Mason gazed at each other with a deep understanding that held neither animosity nor friendship. Gambling and gory memories were all they had in common, and that was enough.

Believing a man should keep his friends close and his enemies closer, Sampson studied Mason. Now prematurely balding, Mason once had a lovely full head of hair before he was captured. Rail thin, Mason fidgeted with his moustache, a well-groomed man with excellent false teeth and pockmarked cheeks. Mason was rumored to have come from a family who owned hundreds of men, women, and children.

"Aren't you going to introduce me to your little friend?" Mason asked Sampson as they settled into the hay.

"Miss Belle Hayden," said Sampson. "Meet Mr. Mason Turner."

Belle shifted uncomfortably as the wagon circled the bonfire.

Sampson inhaled smoky air, chewing a bit of sweet hay.

"Your injury," whispered Belle, "how did it happen?"

Mason laughed and Belle blushed. Sampson did neither. How he hated the questions and stares of friends and strangers alike. Everyone gawked at his stump as if it were the most interesting thing about him.

Every amputation was a story waiting to be told, a sort of mystery, he supposed, and wounded men bled riddles because a soldier's body belonged to everyone. Nothing was private anymore, not to an amputee.

"Mr. Redlaw?" Belle asked. "Major General?"

He thought of how blood seeped through his bandages. The wound, draining, dripped down the stump. Months ago, he developed gangrene. The treatment was why his bone was now exposed under the bandage. He bled for days, like a woman, but he would not tell Belle that, though Mason, Jerry, and Hattie were aware of his condition. Sampson stared at Hattie through the smoke of distant bonfires. She flinched as the wagon jostled over ruts and stones. "I'm not as brave as you think, Miss Belle," he said, thinking himself oozing, mangled, deformed in Hattie's eyes.

"I'm sure you are," said Belle.

Hattie turned toward the dark woods. A coyote howled.

Sampson recalled how the shell had torn off his fingers, exploding, shattering bones as he fell to his knees, crawling along, clawing over bodies of his dying friends, his brothers. Then, the putrid odor of pus, the daily ration of whiskey, multiple surgeries. Mason helped Dr. Burrows split open the stump to remove diseased bone. The fever subsided.

Crickets sang. Wagon wheels crushed branches, fallen leaves. Sampson breathed in the smoke of bonfires and tried to ignore Belle's voice. The child had no understanding of war, nor did he wish to enlighten her. Bats flew overhead. The wagon treaded past woods. A barn owl called. The bright moon lent clarity to misted sky. The scent of hearth fires burning, the delicious spice of pumpkin breads baking, the crisp odor of crushed acorns, fallen leaves blown past houses with jack-o'-lanterns glowing on porch steps.

At the gates of Miss Turner's gracious abode, Sampson stepped off the wagon with Belle. He greeted masked guests, surprisingly chilling to behold. Mostly rabbits, cats, and bats, the masks stirred horror in his heart, though merely cloth, string, paste, wire, papier-mâché, fur, bone, and dried animal skins. The boardinghouse was dark, and the guests were all entering the darkened rooms together full of screams and laughter. He tried smiling at masks of cattle skulls with wigs of horse hair, but bone masks reminded him of what he would rather forget.

Hearth fires, jack-o'-lanterns, and candles lit the matchmaker's house. Sampson stumbled upon couples dancing and singing in the dark music room where dozens of candles burned on the piano. Of all the rooms, only the kitchen was off limits.

"Major General," a woman offered Sampson a goblet of strong hard cider. He followed, losing her in a shadowy hall.

Drinking, listening to whispers on the wind, he followed masked women onto porches.

Later, back inside the house, bathed in hearth light, he told ghostly tales in horrific whispering voices, drunk, pausing only to kiss women in shadows.

"Is that Hawthorne?" he whispered, giggling, pointing to

a silhouette of a man draped in a cape and walking through the dining room, then remembered Hawthorne had died.

After much kissing inspired by ghostly tales, having his nightly fill of parted lips, he wished Miss Turner would turn on the lamps.

What to do with all these superstitions? Women wanted to foretell their future with nut burning, mirror gazing, hoping to see a handsome face smiling back in the glass. Women leaned out windows, listening to whispers on the wind, catching falling leaves for good luck, using salt to repel witches, watching candle flames flicker to gauge the movement of visiting spirits.

Soon, he would have to eat a silent meal at midnight to tempt a spirit to join them at the table. A Christian man, he distrusted the mysticism of the Spiritualist movement. He knew certain women still believed on Halloween they could divine the name or appearance of their future husband by doing tricks with yarn or apple parings. As much as he doubted mediums and séances, he felt pity for those who fell for traps. He thought of the spirit cabinet, a deviant theater where people hoped to reconnect to loved ones beyond the veil.

Inside Miss Turner's boardinghouse, despite its darkness, there was joy.

Sweets and apples hung from strings above doorways. Sampson lifted Belle, and she bit into hanging candies and dangling apples. If the apples were sweet, so would be her love. If the apples were bitter or sour, that was a bad sign, according to Miss Turner.

"Sweet. So sweet," Belle whispered, squiggling as Sampson held her by the waist, lifting her to apples on string as she savored each bite, laughing.

Inside candlelit rooms, Sampson and Belle bobbed for apples before dooking, dropping forks on apples without using hands. They played Puccini, an Irish fortune-telling game using saucers.

"Go, go," said Miss Turner to Belle and Sampson. "In the dark rooms, gaze into my mirrors. The face of future loves will appear. But if a skull appears, you may be destined to die before marriage."

Sampson thought it wrong for Miss Turner to strike terror into the hearts of her boarders, but he supposed it added spice to the night when men and women collided by accident in dark hallways. Belle ran into the room with the big mirror. Lingering near Miss Turner, Sampson was careful to avoid that room.

Every time Belle thrilled, squealing shrilly from the dark, Sampson wondered what it meant.

"Has she seen the handsome face or the skull?" he asked.

"Why don't you ask her?" Ruby teased, daring him to enter the room. Of course, he wouldn't because Belle might see his face in the mirror and get the wrong impression.

7

Willa stared into the boardinghouse windows, lit by jack-o'-lanterns. Faces of carved pumpkins glowed like the Halloween balls at Turner Plantation, once called Twin Oaks because so many children born into that estate were identical twins. Willa thought of them and shuddered, realizing the only thing worse than having a twin sister who had died was having one who would never die.

The plantation's first twin mediums were now old women estranged from each other—one rumored to be dead, the other hiding her ties to Twin Oaks. Ruby, an elderly, prosperous abolitionist, resided in Concord, Massachusetts. Her twin Clara had continued living in Tennessee at Twin Oaks until the mansion was destroyed by fire during the Civil War.

Willa, who had escaped Twin Oaks during the war, had made it to Ruby's house. As she gazed into the windows, Willa was shocked to see Clara hiding among the guests.

Clara, first rumored to have died decades ago when an oil lamp caught her dress on fire, was often seen at Spiritualist gatherings, where her fire-scarred hands directed processions of young mediums. The second time she was rumored to die by fire was during the uprising at Twin Oaks. The third and most recent rumor of her death was months ago in Boston, a possible murder-suicide. Newspapers reported she had burned in an apartment fire with two others in another attempt to contact the dead.

However, no newspaper ever reported the tragedy of the two lovely teenage twin mediums from Twin Oaks, Valerie and Maggie. Freedwomen like Willa, Maggie and Valerie were still together, devoted to each other and trying to find a place to live after Valerie's murder. Willa had heard that Clara murdered Valerie, though Valerie refused to die. Valerie and Clara were alike that way, both causing trouble even after they died, both making appearances when everyone assumed they should not be among the living.

Like Ruby and Clara, Valerie and Maggie were identical twins born on the plantation. Unlike Ruby and Clara, Valerie and Maggie had not been free.

Willa wondered if death wasn't as permanent as most people believed. She wondered if twins were susceptible to haunting each other and if twins born on Twin Oaks plantation were likely to cross boundaries once free of their bodies. Was Clara really dead? If she was dead, could she still cause harm? During a séance, could a medium erase boundaries between herself and her twin just as she erased boundaries between the living and the dead?

Gazing intently through the boardinghouse windows, Willa braced herself for what might happen, knowing she couldn't stay on the outside for long. At first, she couldn't believe what she was seeing. Through the windows, Willa saw Valerie, Maggie, and Clara, all seeming to be very much alive. Clara bobbed for apples. Maggie pushed Valerie in a wheelchair. The three of them seemed to be having a wonderful time. Willa wondered how it was possible. Having escaped Twin Oaks' burning rooms, all the women from Twin Oaks somehow found their way into Ruby's Halloween party, mingling with invited guests and camouflaged among masked revelers in the dark.

Women in masks explored candlelit rooms with men in uniform who lifted the women so they could bite into apples spinning from strings dangling from doorways. Sneaking to the edge of the sleeping porch, hovering near an open door, Willa listened. One voice stood out from the others. In the past, many times before, it gave her chills at the old plantation where a beautiful indigo mold grew in the high corners of the wallpaper.

The singsong voice pleaded with another voice, also familiar, though less so.

The voice Willa would never forget, one she felt inside her

body before recognizing it.

She couldn't place the other voice until a laughing woman removed her mask near candlelight, flames on the piano illuminating fiery red curls and spattering of freckles.

Willa knew she had to get inside the boardinghouse.

The boardinghouse filled with waves of laughter, cheers, and applause, men and women playing silly games. Willa hoped her bloody dress looked like a Halloween costume. If only she had a mask to cover her face, she would blend into the party nicely, her amputation hidden beneath tattered shawl. Gently, she stroked the skin flap stitched over her wrist and recalled how Mason worked to save her.

And there he was. Standing behind the piano, drinking from a copper mug.

She was about to run away, behind the boardinghouse, when she saw a woman drop a butterfly mask on the leaves. Shadow concealed the woman's face as Willa snatched the mask before the woman realized.

Hiding her face behind the butterfly and tucking her left wrist inside her shawl, Willa snuck into the boardinghouse to search for any evidence of Godfrey.

Slipping past parlor games, gliding through the couples, Willa navigated the dark stairs. She knew she didn't have much time. Finding a single candle burning on a hallstand, Willa grabbed it and began opening doors. Finally, she discovered Viv's room. She knew right away when she saw the huge cameras, their large boxy silhouettes in candlelight. The cameras took up most of the room, so it was hard to find a little narrow path to walk around the slim bed.

Shutting the door behind her, she waved the candle to illuminate nooks and crannies, starting with the wardrobe. The doors were stuck, so she had to force them open with a splintering of wood. Willa held her breath and worried someone might hear. A woman's laughter echoed in the dark behind her. Gazing back, Willa saw a shadow but thought the laughter must be coming from another room.

Tossing Viv's things on the wooden floor, ripping gowns and boxes out of the wardrobe, she moved the candle away from the wardrobe, close to the bed, where an unlit oil lamp sat on a locked chest of drawers.

With her full weight, she pulled the locked drawer and the chest moved inches before she fell backwards, bruising herself, shattering the oil lamp. Her body went numb, sensing something wrong. She worried she would catch fire. It was easy to do with spilt oil and candle flame. She thought of Clara Turner.

She heard the laughter again, from the dark corner, this time unmistakable. Tempted to run out of the room, she turned to face the corner. Slowly, ever so slowly, emerged a woman wearing a black veil. Heavy mourning hid her face. Swallowing hard, Willa took a deep breath and moved her candle toward the woman.

The laughter transformed into a maniacal cackle as the woman raised her black veil to reveal her face, wan and elegant, but unwell, too thin. Willa recognized her as one of the plantation's unfortunate twin enslaved girls, the identical twins who once worked as mediums for Clara Turner. Willa had heard that Valerie's murder happened as a result of Clara's demanding she perform the trick of birthing spirits called "materializations." Before Spiritualist demonstrations, Clara forced objects inside girls' throats, nostrils, and vaginas. Sometimes cutting off airways, Clara stuffed larger and larger drawings, cotton wads, and fabric swatches, even offal inside of Valerie. At the séance, to her audience's horror, Valerie was strangled by the materialization caught inside her throat, while she birthed a materialization.

Maggie sat with her twin sister's body for months, locked away in a distant room of the octagonal plantation mansion with vast imposing porches linking outer walls with white pillars like bleached bone in sunlight. Maggie walked the porches, telling anyone who would listen that her murdered sister was still alive. Willa knew dead was dead. It scared her when Maggie began to call herself Valerie.

Willa could never tell the twins apart. God rest one of their souls, whichever one it might be. She prayed, shaking, her arms covered in goose pimples as she recalled both pale girls: wild eyes, long swanlike necks, wet-looking ebony hair straightened with chemical tonic. Wearing fish-scale-colored skirts and flesh-colored blouses, they had the look of mermaids in the twilight of the séance room.

Perhaps the twins had been so close to each other that it drove the surviving twin to the brink of insanity, or past the brink, outliving her sister.

Clara Turner's Spiritualism meant for the twins that death was not a separation. She taught them to believe the dead could still speak, but Willa often thought the sisters misunderstood, especially the sister who had lived. Clara Turner taught her to believe she could speak to her dead sister beyond the veil. This only worsened the situation, so that things progressed far beyond what Clara had intended. Willa remembered the horror of those nights—the way the living sister refused to let go of the murdered sister. Much to Clara Turner's dismay, the living sister disappeared shortly after sneaking the body of her twin away.

"Absconding with the dead," said Clara, "I thought she was raised better."

Willa feared the day she would discover what had happened to the twins. Not much terrified her but that did.

She knew she had to face it now. It wasn't this girl's fault. Clara Turner toyed with all vulnerable girls, especially twins.

"Maggie?" Willa whispered. "Is that you?"

"No," the standing woman said.

"Valerie?" asked Willa, moving the candle toward the darkness beside the young woman, who pointed downward, to her left.

The candle trembled, light wavering before Willa shone it on the twin to reveal a woman in a wheelchair, camouflaged by heavy mourning—black gloves, long black dress, and black veil covering her face. In her gloved hands, she held a box.

"Please take it," said the standing woman.

Willa still wasn't sure if she was Valerie or Maggie. Why did she say she was Valerie? Willa thought maybe Valerie was the twin who had been murdered. Maybe it wasn't Maggie. Or was it? Maggie or Valerie, Willa tried to remember. But who sat in the wheelchair? Maggie? Valerie? The possibilities spun wildly through Willa's head. The uncertainty terrified her, her pity mingling with revulsion. An even worse possibility occurred to her: what if the woman in the wheelchair was Clara Turner? What if Clara had lived through another fire and resumed her work with the twins?

Reaching for the wooden box, Willa struggled to hold the candle and the box in her right hand. She placed the box on the bed, the candle on the chest of drawers, balanced in a pool of melted wax. Opening the box, she discovered an object wound in gauze. It had a chemical smell. Unwinding the gauze, she screamed to discover she was holding a hand—it was her own left hand, withered yet preserved.

Dropping the hand near the wheelchair, Willa couldn't bear the memories it brought back. It was dead and hard and cold, no longer a part of her. Her hand had fed her and scratched her itches. It had wiped the sweat from her lips. It had bathed her and carried cool palmfuls of water to her thirsty tongue. Her hand didn't deserve to die, but she had sacrificed it when she was only a teenager, whacking her wrist repeatedly with a long sharp knife, slicing flesh from bone. The only way to stop those who traded enslaved women from selling her at auction was the cutting. Blood spurted like a hot spring erupting into the auctioneers' faces.

The woman in the wheelchair began to put on a show. She waved her hand at Willa while twitching her fingers until they danced like spiders. Willa watched in amazement as her dead hand began to twitch and dance, mimicking the motion of the woman's hand. The woman in the wheelchair called to the dead hand. It stilled at her voice before scampering toward her on its fingers. It leapt into her lap like a kitten as she petted it.

Willa ran out of the room, rushing into the dark hall so fast she smacked into a wall, knocking off several portraits. She stumbled and then ran into guests before darting out of the house.

Leaping off the porch, Willa dropped the butterfly mask and darted toward the safety of the dark woods. On the edge of the trees, two men stood, dressed in dark costumes camouflaged by night. She thought they were merely shadows and ran toward them, crashing into them. One man was dressed as a warlock and the other man wore a grinning bone mask. They caught her. She couldn't escape their grasp. They began to hold her down. She fought, but they were too strong. Before she realized what was happening, they were saying her name.

The man in the bone mask removed his mask to reveal Godfrey's face.

Willa leapt into his arms. They embraced while she recalled how she feared she would never see him again.

8.

Holding a candle so golden light wavered over her face, Belle Hayden descended the boardinghouse stairs. Jerry held his breath. A hush enveloped the room.

With raven hair, long and straight, a delicate beauty mark on her chin, a shapely high bosom, and slender hips swishing in her skirts, Belle appeared to float where she walked. The singed dress made her more alluring by candlelight. Jerry stared. She stared back, only long enough. Peach-colored lips and cheeks, blue veins on her wrists, pale translucent skin, she was called "the little girl" for her tiny frame and delicate features. Apparently, she had contracted yellow fever as a child and stopped growing, almost died, being of delicate health because her dentist treated her with mercury when she was teething. She suffered terrible headaches that sent her to bed for days. Thinking of her warm brown eyes, Jerry wished he had the chance to soothe her pain.

If only he had been more patient. If only he hadn't been so willing to betray Sampson! Now it was too late. Even though Hattie's pregnancy wasn't showing, Jerry suspected he would have a daughter.

Removing her butterfly mask, Hattie pulled Jerry into a corner to kiss his lips as she whispered, "I had a visit from my friend today."

"What friend?" Jerry asked, disgusted, trying to gaze over Hattie's hair to spy on Belle as she moved from one shadowy corner to another. Damn it! He was losing her.

An entire year going from one Confederate hellhole to another. Enduring imprisonment, only to be trapped by the first woman he had called on when he was finally back home! Being near Hattie now gave him the sensation of the illness he suffered in Andersonville when he first heard tales of the death list.

"The woman in the red dress, Jerry," whispered Hattie.

Exasperated, Jerry thought of every woman who wore red. Easily confused, he was never quite right after prison, having suffered the lasting impact of trauma and confinement, not to mention starvation, dysentery, hookworm, scurvy, opium, and maltreatment.

Hattie whispered, "I'm not pregnant!"

His heart stopped beating, only for a moment. He wasn't sure he had heard correctly. Had he escaped another prison?

"Tell your friend," Jerry said, "she has made me the happiest man in the world."

Hattie dropped her mask on the hardwood floor. "What do you mean?" she whispered.

Not knowing how to say what he must without hurting her, Jerry tried not to let his happiness show but he needed to be honest to make a clean escape, saying, "I thought your friend had forsaken you because of me. Now she's back?"

"Well, yes," said Hattie. "So she is. She's funny that way. Now, you and I have all the time in the world to enjoy our wedding, to really do things right."

"I don't know, Hattie. Are we really doing the right thing?"

"What do you mean?"

"Weren't we getting married for the sake of the child?"

"We can have another," Hattie said, her voice breaking.

"Let's call off our engagement? Take some time and think on it. We were wrong to do what we did to Sampson. Maybe he'll forgive us, enough to take you back?"

"What makes you think I want him back?" asked Hattie.

"You were engaged to Sampson before our mistake?"

"I want to marry you."

"Hattie, please. We made a mistake. Now, we have a second chance. I didn't even get a chance to think about what I wanted."

"How could you not know?" asked Hattie.

"I do now," said Jerry.

"What then?"

"I want you to release me." Jerry gently reached down to hold Hattie's hand, caressing her fingers. "Please, Hattie."

"Consider yourself released," said Hattie, weeping silently. Jerry let go of her hand.

As if on cue, Miss Ruby Turner lit her lamps and the room filled with golden light. Jerry's eyes adjusted. He struggled to focus on Hattie's face. Was she still crying? Wiping away tears? She quickly donned the butterfly mask.

As his appetite suddenly returned, Jerry inhaled deeply and gazed upon the long table decorated with a massive cobweb of yarn. The room filled with the scent of roasted meat and freshly baked bread. A feast for the eyes, decorated in the style of a dusty candlelit cathedral, communion goblets gleamed at each empty chair. At the head of the table, Jerry studied the throne reserved for the invisible guest.

Kora placed trays of delectable food before him on the table. Speaking in an Irish accent, wearing a maid's uniform, she smiled at him and the other guests often. Petite with large bright green eyes and silky chestnut curls tied up in a knot, Kora was strong and hardworking, rumored to be double-jointed because of all the gymnastics she did in the garden. Twitching her thin dark eyebrows, Kora moved jauntily in the style of a woman who loves music. She had a pale powdery complexion like white cake, but she colored easily when angry. Jerry adored Kora for her rich chocolate curls. Energetic with her tiny dainty feet, she was well versed about the superstitions of her old country, especially Irish dumb suppers. As tiny as she was, she enjoyed cooking large traditional meals. She loved pets and trinkets and found objects and creatures from the woods. She also loved Chris Datchery, but their on-and-off romance was something of a badly kept secret.

"Let's begin," Miss Ruby Turner said. "Remove your masks. I'll introduce everyone and go over the rules of the dumb supper."

The guests removed their masks, hung them on hooks on

the wall, as Jerry tried not to look at Hattie's naked face, bathed in tears.

"Once we sit at the table, no talking, or noise of any kind. This chair," Miss Turner said, pointing to the throne at the head of the table, "remains empty for our invisible guest. The spirit of one who has died will join us only if we remain silent. Understood?"

Jerry nodded.

Women giggled and Mason shushed them.

"Now, did you remember to bring what I asked?"

"What, Miss Turner?" Chris Datchery asked.

"A note—a secret note—a question you wish to ask of someone who is dead. Keep it folded, put away, hidden on your person, all during the supper. Never tell a soul what's written on the paper. After we eat, we'll take turns burning these notes by candlelight."

"What if I forgot?" asked Chris.

Miss Turner revealed several sheets of paper, before passing the paper and pencils around the room. Jerry tucked his note inside his jacket pocket. Chris and Henry, as well as a few of the women, hastily scribbled on the paper. Sampson Redlaw also began to write.

Miss Turner gestured to everyone to take their places at the table. Each place was labeled with a name card to leave nothing to chance. Jerry was seated in an undistinguished side chair, right beside Hattie. Sampson was seated in an oversized rustically carved chair, nestled between Grace and Belle Hayden. Viv sat near Dr. Burrows, and Aria was seated near Chris Datchery and Mason Turner.

"Now, I'll make introductions, starting with soldiers recently returned from war," said Miss Turner. "Among our heroes, the most decorated, Major General Sampson Redlaw."

Sampson bowed.

"And our very own Dr. Burrows, who saved so many lives on the battlefield, assisted by Mason Turner." Mason and Dr. Burrows nodded to each other and then smiled at Miss Turner.

"Of course, we could never forget our brave schoolteacher also returned from war, Nick Dalton," said Ruby, gesturing tenderly to Nick, who clutched his wooden leg beneath the table. "And our young solider, Jerry Rickett, golden haired and starry eyed as ever."

Several women tittered.

"And our brave Chris Datchery."

"Now for the rest of us. My dear elder brother, Henry Turner. My friend, Miss Florence Green. And my indispensable cook and maid, Kora."

Everyone cheered for Kora loudest of all.

"And, of course, my boarders, the Hayden sisters, daughters of my dear recently deceased childhood friend, Lara Hayden." Miss Turner gazed longingly at the empty throne. "They are, in order of their birth, Aria, Grace, Belle, and Viv. All very single."

"That's not everyone," said Henry. "You forgot someone important, besides the priest!"

Jerry laughed as several surprise guests stepped out from behind the dining room doorway.

"Oh?" asked Miss Turner. "Father Hayden? I didn't realize."

"Wouldn't miss it for the world," Michael Hayden said.

Jerry looked round to see how many more chairs would be needed. Though food was more than abundant, chairs were another matter, so it was a relief to see one of the ladies was an invalid who had brought her own chair on wheels.

"The twins!" Henry called out, gesturing to the invalid and her attendant, whom Jerry guessed must be her sister.

"Who?" asked Miss Turner.

"We have in our attendance tonight the famous Usherwood twins, understudies of the late great Spiritualist, our long-lost sister, Miss Clara Turner."

Jerry noticed Mason's eyes grow wide.

The two fragile teenage girls waited behind Henry, one in the wheelchair, her face covered in a dark mourning veil so

Jerry could not see her features. The starved-looking twins were in stark contrast to Henry's corpulence, his suit buttons straining. Jerry wondered if the twins were identical but had no way of determining because the healthy sister was the caretaker of the invalid, the veiled.

"But you're Maggie and Valerie?" asked Mason. "I remember when you were girls. I thought one of you died?"

"No," said the standing twin. "That was an unfortunate rumor in the chaos of the war. There are many people who are very much alive who you assume are dead."

"Is that so? Who else?" asked Mason.

"Please, don't stare," said the standing twin.

"I apologize," said Mason. "I was only surprised and now very grateful to know you are both still with us."

"Very well," said the standing twin.

Mason nodded.

"Sir?" the twin who stood now said to Jerry, who was staring at the girl in the wheelchair. "We are guests of the party, not putting on a show."

"Apologies, ladies," Jerry whispered. "I was just wondering if you are identical twins? It's impossible to tell with the veil."

"My sister does not remove her veil," said the standing twin. "Nor does she speak."

"You speak for her, Miss?"

"I am the speaker, Maggie Usherwood," said the standing twin, speaking with assurance as she gently placed her hand upon her veiled sister's wheelchair. "My sister, Valerie, is the veiled. Her veil is her silence and all you cannot see."

"What does that mean?" asked Jerry.

"They are mediums," said Henry with great pride as he gestured to the twins. "Sisters of Séance. Valerie never leaves her chair, though she can move farther with greater speed than any of us. She moves so quickly we can't see her moving."

"Her?" asked Ruby, staring at the slight and unmoving veiled twin in the wheelchair. "She moves? Where? How?"

"She ventures beyond the veil to communicate with the dead who magnetize to her," said Henry. "She travels to other worlds by staying still. She speaks to entities by remaining silent. Though she seems alone but for Maggie, she is constantly surrounded by friends because the dead are always with her. All around her, every hour, is a party of spirits we cannot see unless she shows them through séance."

A strange mix of pity and horror washed over Jerry as he beheld the dark-veiled creature in the wheelchair, though he was glad she had her own chair, so he wouldn't have to give up his.

"Mediums?" asked Belle as Chris Datchery dragged in extra chairs. "Will there be a séance?"

"Not tonight," said Miss Turner. "Certainly not."

"Clara Turner?" asked Florence Green. "I've heard the name before, in the papers. Something unpleasant. Surely, she wasn't related to our Miss Turner!"

A tight smile cracked on Viv's lips.

"Let's not talk about that. Not tonight," said Henry.

"The fire with—"

"Florence, not in front of her daughters," said Kora.

"Whose daughters?" asked Florence. "Clara Turner didn't have any daughters. Did she?"

"True," said the standing twin in her clear bell-like voice. "Clara Turner had no children but was like a mother to many, including my sister and me. She was murdered in the same fire that killed Lara Hayden, mother to some of the women here. It has been in all the papers, Miss Green."

"Usherwood," said Ruby, "that is a strange name."

"We chose it ourselves," said the twin who stood.

"But why?" asked Florence.

"We ran away from Clara and didn't want anyone finding us. Not wanting to take the name of our former captors, we chose a name of our own."

Jerry remembered reading about it or, rather, his mother reading the article full of hearsay. Clara Turner was merely a fraud, a hoax to get desperate mourners to part with money, a monster motivated by a need for attention and greed. Like most monsters, she had religious precedents. The Spiritualist community had created the perfect environment for her performances. The devout swore she was the real thing. At her performances, one twin would die and the living twin would then speak to her dead sister through séance, or become one with her dead twin in the spirit cabinet, where they could share the same body. Like any authentic materialization, it was a hideous and sometimes pathetic demonstration, requiring an actual living body in the form of a medium willing to give birth to a spirit, or spirits, publicly and often. Some mediums birthed litters.

"My sister and I are investigating Clara's death, using spirits guides, who brought us here." Maggie added, "We can't thank Mr. Turner enough for allowing us as his guests."

"Henry!" Miss Ruby Turner said.

"I thought this was a Halloween party," said Sampson, "not a murder investigation."

While some of the men snickered, Henry and Ruby were not smiling. Neither was Sampson.

"Shall we go?" whispered Hattie, discretely reaching for Jerry's hand.

He moved away from her.

"No," he said, thinking the night was just getting interesting, curious to know how this connected to Belle. What happened that night her mother died in the fire with Miss Clara Turner?

Henry Turner addressed the group as if he were a lecturer at Town Hall, though no one had asked him to speak. "Followers of the Spiritualist movement do participate in séances where mediums try to contact the dead. Dumb suppers are also held, in which participants eat dinner in complete silence with extra places to encourage spirits to sit at the table. But tonight's supper is just a game. Ruby didn't even know the twins would be here. If anyone is to blame, it's me."

"As usual," said Ruby.

Nick Dalton gestured to the twins. "They're here. That changes everything, especially for devout Catholics." Nick gave a meaningful look directed toward Father Michael Hayden.

Jerry stared at Nick, the handsome schoolteacher who had lost his right leg in the war. Nick wore a prosthetic. Prematurely gray with silver strands that sparkled in a metallic manner, he possessed a full head of hair. Nick was debonair, graceful yet stiff. Otherwise, the prosthetic leg under his clothes wasn't noticeable. He didn't like to talk about his leg or how he lost it. With bright rose lips and elfin ears beneath his hair, his narrow sparkling eyes were not those of a man's man. Wearing glasses, even when he was walking late at night, Nick moved as quietly as the wildcat in the woods.

Nick nodded to Jerry, who realized he was staring.

"What bothers me," the priest said in a measured tone, "is the connection between Spiritualism and the occult." Michael Hayden bowed his head, as if studying his polished shoes. "I'm sorry to say, Miss Ruby, I cannot play this sort of game."

"Understood," said Ruby, who gasped as if realizing how much understood sounded like Usherwood.

"I apologize," said Father Hayden, stepping toward the door.

"No need. Would anyone else like to leave?" Ruby looked toward Henry and the twins, who said nothing. "I would certainly understand."

Henry helped the priest gather his hat, scarf, cane, and gloves at the hallstand before Father Michael Hayden exited, looking back with a rueful smile at Ruby.

"I assure you," Henry turned to address the room. "My sister had no idea the twins were coming. Ruby's dumb supper is just a dinner party."

"And this empty chair is reserved for?" asked Dr. Burrows, pointing to the throne.

"No one has been tricked, save me by my brother," said Ruby.

"Wonderful," said Chris Datchery. "I'm starved."

"Bring your notes to the table," said Miss Turner. "Any secret question you wish to ask deceased loved ones. At the end of the supper, these notes must be burned by candle flame."

"Very well, Miss Turner," said Jerry, gazing at the sickly veiled twin in the wheelchair.

The twins refused to sit at the table, waiting behind it, refusing food. The rest of the women were paired with men at the table, the empty throne at the table's head, opposite Miss Turner. The guests solemnly obeyed Miss Turner's rules, sitting in silence, enjoying their meal, clutching their private notes to the dead, until they began to fall into moments of inexplicable hilarity. The twins never laughed, but kept staring at the empty throne as laughter, contagious, moved in waves, erupting from one end of the table to the other.

Since conversation was forbidden, Jerry was grateful the food was intense and plentiful since everyone had to watch each other eating in silence. However, he found the dinner rather confusing. As with all traditional dumb suppers, the courses were served backwards, so that the meal started with dessert and coffee, moved on to the entrée, then soup, salad, and finally the dinner rolls and appetizers. Jerry tried to create a scheme where he re-reversed the order by collecting his food on his plate, hiding some of it in his pockets, in his lap, beneath the table, so that he could then reorder his courses to eat them in proper order. However, with each newly added course, Miss Turner and Kora kept the old course on the table, so that the circle of edibles seemed never ending, chaotic but unbroken. To add to the confusion of his food hoarding, the silverware was placed backwards and upside down, as was traditional. It was enough to make his head spin. He really had to concentrate on what he was doing, to avoid making a fool of himself, but ended up dropping food on his clothes and the rug.

The sensual possibilities delighted him, despite the awkwardness. He loved novelty. Kora had gone to much trouble, preparing stock of lean veal, beef, and hambone. Fresh soft-shelled crabs, sandbags removed, shaggy fried in hot oil. Jerry gorged on fresh bread and cheese with orchard wine, lobster, and oyster stuffing. Tartines, sweet goose, little hens, dried figs, and white bean soup paired with a delicate white sauce, butter and flour bubbling into cups of cream. He knew how women enjoyed making white sauce, how they enjoyed eating it, how he enjoyed watching them eating it, but memories of the white ooze of séances put Spiritualists off it, especially with the Usherwood twins sitting near the table.

Jerry wondered if when he was an old man, he would realize he had witnessed love's history over candlelight at dinner parties. He had attended so many, each one marking a passage in the social life of people meeting, courting, marrying, starting families, hosting more dinner parties over time.

Long red candles burnt, golden light dancing over cherry water glasses catching falling hothouse petals. At first, it seemed merely a pretty table display. Later, as Jerry watched roses falling apart, he hoped it wasn't an omen. He felt Hattie looking at him and wondered if an apology was in order, but he could never risk the peace by giving it.

Jerry stared at the empty throne and wondered why silence was thought to preserve the connection to the dead. Did the dead like silence? Maybe the silence wasn't for the dead but for the living—to force them to listen to what they normally wouldn't hear. To remain in communication with death while feasting, the guests were to practice nonverbal communication. Silence brought them closer together. A more intimate and innate communication took over when they couldn't rely on words. Bonding while eating, they often patted their pockets where notes were tucked away— *secrets, secrets,* such gestures teased as they smiled at each other's questioning glances.

Realizing he had escaped the responsibility of fatherhood, Jerry had a wonderful time, wondering what everyone had written to a dead person he or she once knew. Grinning at each other, the guests seemed to hunger for secrets more than food. Secrets were delicious, he thought, guessing the contents of the notes. At the end of the supper, if the notes really were to be burned by candle flame without being shared in some way, Jerry thought it a pity. A missed opportunity.

The ceiling thundered and the women's faces filled with terror. Tapping resounded behind the house's walls. Jerry looked to the twins' gloved hands clearly displayed. Each guest sought to reassure the others, displaying hands and shoes. Everyone gazed at each other with wide eyes. As mysteriously as the tapping began, it ceased.

Miss Turner gathered everyone around candles in her parlor. Removing a small folded scrap of paper from her skirt pocket, holding the paper over the flame of the candle, she allowed the paper to smolder in her gloved hand. The flame leapt to her fingers. She dropped the paper onto a porcelain plate, where it burnt to ash.

Jerry Rickett clutched the note he had brought to the party—a secret question he had written to his ancestor, a magistrate who played a role in the Salem witchcraft hysteria. His great-great-grand uncle believed in the power of certain women to afflict others through magic dolls called poppets. Having sentenced many witches to die after witch-cake tests, he was cursed by one of the condemned as she walked to the gallows.

One by one, guests burned their notes by candle flame.

Jerry waited until last.

After burning his note, Jerry looked to Belle and prayed that Sampson wouldn't look at her, not the way she was looking at him. Jerry couldn't take his eyes off her, didn't know what to do. Her magnificent dark gleaming curls. The sweetness of her gaze, intense yet shy. Already, her eyes resisted, refusing to meet his. Usually, he could attract women with just a look. Women flocked to him like pollinators to honey. He usually shooed them away, not wanting to harm them. Now, with Belle and his new freedom, things changed. Her pale coloring and dark hair were like the Usherwood twins, but her charms markedly different. Her skin seemed to glow, smooth and luminous like milk glass under gaslight, set off by the chocolate tones of her moody brown eyes.

Hattie glared at him, her eyes like daggers.

He averted her stare and met the twins'. Maggie smirked and her expression made his blood curdle as he pondered what made the twins appear disturbing. Or perhaps disturbed. He wondered if people appeared disturbing to others because they were disturbed people. If so, this was a sad aspect of human nature, since those in need of compassion might be the very ones who horrified those they needed most. Judging by the stiff unmoving hands on her wheelchair, Valerie appeared deathlier than a woman in a postmortem.

Fire reflected in Belle's dark eyes. Jerry began cracking his knuckles to get her attention, drawing a severe look from Miss Turner, who said, "So concludes our ceremony."

"The silence is broken?" whispered Nick. "But we haven't received the answers?"

"Ask the twins," said Henry.

"Open your minds, open your hearts, listen to this thing you call silence. It is full of voices that go unheard," the standing twin said, leaving the room without explanation.

"Miss Usherwood?" Jerry whispered, feeling afraid something was wrong with Valerie but not daring to approach her wheelchair. "Valerie?"

"Wait," said Henry. "Where's Maggie?"

Maggie had abandoned Valerie, who slumped over in the wheelchair as if sleeping.

"Come, Jerry Rickett," said Miss Turner. "I want to find where she went."

"This way," said Jerry, glimpsing the dining room. Maggie stood beside the empty throne reserved for the invisible guest. She chattered profusely, agitated, as if in intense conversation, though no one sat in the throne. At first, he thought she was arguing, then he realized she was negotiating.

"There's no one," Jerry said to Maggie.

"A ghost! Miss Usherwood is speaking to a ghost," whispered Belle to Jerry and her sisters, gazing behind the parlor doorway. Jerry winked at her.

"There's a woman sitting here," said Maggie. "I see her plain as day."

"What's she doing?" Jerry laughed, wondering if she were teasing him, flirting.

"Asking for you, Jerry," said Maggie.

Muffled laughter erupted from the party guests, though Ruby seemed rather serious in questioning Maggie. Jerry wondered if this was planned as an elaborate game set up by his host.

"What?" asked Miss Turner. "What do you mean she's asking for Mr. Rickett? Who is she, and what can she want with the boy?"

In the sweetest voice, Maggie answered, "She's playing with her doll collection, her poppets. She's happy because her poppets are always with her, talking. Her poppets are saying Jerry's uncle, the magistrate, is choking on witch cakes in hell."

"What?" asked Miss Turner, leaning into the cupboard as if she might fall.

Jerry grasped her left arm to steady her. "It's alright," he whispered. "It doesn't bother me at all. It's just a game. Isn't it, Miss Usherwood?"

Laughter in the parlor grew silent. Jerry gazed through the doorway to glimpse Belle dropping a bonbon cake onto a saucer as Grace began coughing, unable to swallow a bit of bonbon she had slipped into her mouth. Aria whacked Grace on the back to stop her choking as Grace, unable to breathe, flung the dessert off her plate. A small white dog ran through the room and caught the bonbon cake that flew from Grace's mouth.

"Oh, no," said Belle, "don't let the dog eat that!"

Aria patted Grace's back.

Grace attempted to regain her composure as the dog ran through the parlor.

Ruby Turner and Jerry gazed at the dog eating the cake and then stared into each other's eyes. The dog ran to Maggie Usherwood.

"Where did that little dog come from?" asked Jerry.

"I'm sure I don't know," said Ruby. "Perhaps it's hers?"

"Well, someone must have invited it to the party," said Sampson.

Maggie laughed and the dog licked her gloved hands.

Jerry recalled the talk of superstitious people baking witch cakes with urine and rye flour before feeding the cake to dogs to ferret out witches. How appropriate for Halloween, yet how unwelcome. He had never been so unhappy to see a dog.

"Wonderful party, Miss Turner," Maggie Usherwood beamed at the little dog as if simply delighted.

"Come on, Miss Turner," said Jerry, leading Ruby away as the dog began to bark, leaping into Maggie's lap.

Finding a comfortable chair for Miss Turner, Jerry hung back as Sampson gathered the Hayden sisters around him, taking up the entire sofa, facing Grace on her high-backed chair. In the little rocking chair, Belle laughed softly.

As usual, Sampson had a bawdy sense of humor. Belle apparently didn't understand, but the other women, especially Grace, appeared to understand all too well.

Sampson focused on Grace Hayden, despite the mortifying things he was saying. Grace, of all the sisters, possessed the least tolerance for indecorum. A taller woman, her cold eyes offset lean features in precise symmetry. Her form and face imposing, she was a reserved woman unlikely to be charmed by any soldier's tales. Sampson seemed clueless, as Jerry watched him commit social suicide.

"One morning," Sampson said, "I had been searching houses for deserters and found a doctor under a girl's bed, claiming to cure gonorrhea."

"What is gonorrhea?" asked Belle. "I think I've heard of it."

"Have you?"

Jerry sighed. It was common for prostitutes to enter army camps, claiming to be sisters or wives of soldiers. Sampson's duty to his country somehow left him time for recreation with patriotic women who visited every few nights, among them a notorious whore he once introduced as his wife.

"Had gonorrhea as a boy, long before the war," Sampson said, winking at Grace before clearing his throat for emphasis, "and cured it myself."

"You'll put me out of business," said Dr. Burrows, laughing.

"This might." Sampson held up his amputation for all to see.

Drunk as a skunk, again, thought Jerry.

Belle drew nearer to Sampson, hovering over him. The worse he behaved, the more she devoured him with loving eyes.

"These ladies came to my tent at a whistle," said Sampson.

Dear God, Jerry wondered, what was that smell? The stench of a caged animal! Was it . . . Sampson? Sitting among ladies, talking of whores, smoking a fat cigar while telling how he cured himself of gonorrhea in childhood, Sampson probably hadn't bathed in months. How did he get away with it? Likely by drinking too much whiskey.

Jerry envied Sampson his visible wound, realizing it made him a hero. As Belle laughed softly, Jerry wished he had been lucky enough to lose a hand in the war. He remembered Sampson leading the men to battle—at 6'4" with an impressive mane of reddish hair and hazel eyes, in an army of short men with dark complexions, Sampson was hard to overlook.

Realizing how deeply offended and repulsed Grace Hayden appeared, Jerry took heart, thinking Belle soon would realize how disgusting Sampson was. The more Sampson spoke, the more Grace appeared to recoil from him, as if he suffered from a contagious disease. Sampson lit a cigar and Grace reared back like a frightened pony. He closed his eyes and tilted his head back, flinging his mane as lice scattered. Eyes still closed, Sampson began exhaling perfect smoke rings toward the ceiling.

"Everyone says you're a hero," said Belle.

Sampson paused, mid-inhalation, opened his eyes.

"Everyone's a fool," said Sampson, scratching the back of his head and flicking lice off his shoulders. "People aren't vermin. A man can't go about slaughtering them because they get in the way."

"That's exactly what a soldier does. He becomes an exterminator of men," said Mason.

Sampson nodded his shaggy head and Jerry wondered how many Union Officers had been slaughtered by Mason.

"I never thought that," said Belle.

"Sampson was one of the best," said Mason.

"War is no excuse," said Grace. Setting her cup and saucer on the lamp table, she rose from her chair. Sampson reached out to assist her but she slipped past him. "Belle, show Mr. Rickett your projects," said Grace. "Thank you all for a pleasant evening. Especially you, Miss Turner."

Standing at the parlor doorway, silent in shadows, Miss Turner had been quietly observing. "Sweet dreams, Grace," she said. "And Belle, dear, entertain us with your art. Mr. Rickett would be quite charmed, I'm sure."

"Our Belle has quite the talent for memorial sculpture," said Aria, the goat-faced sister. "She spins lovely flowers."

"True," said Viv, her fiery red hair falling against her green dress. Jerry thought Viv a worldly eccentric with jaded eyes, a bit too plump of breast and belly.

Aria touched the piano keys as if music were second nature. She possessed a piano player's hands, long graceful fingers with an impressive reach and control. Fingers dancing over the keys, she was an odd-looking woman with bright blue eyes. Although no one would call her a beauty, he could tell she was greatly talented and loved—a top-heavy woman but with an intoxicating smile and fascinating animated eyes. She winked at him. Scribbling song lyrics and musical notes, composing as she played, she kept a pencil tucked behind her ear.

Belle reached into the window seat for her crafting basket. Sorting several satchels, she displayed two silkily gleaming ebony roses resting on her ivory palms. She offered dark petals to each person in the parlor.

The twins lingered in a corner in silence, not quite part of the group. Hattie Grove was also sitting away, alone, trying to hide her tears, touching her face with her gloves and dredging up an occasional fake laugh.

"Black roses," said Jerry.

"Memorial art," said Belle.

"It is our duty to properly mourn the dead. And create beauty out of pain," said Viv.

Jerry followed Belle around the room. "Will you show me more?"

"Someday," said Belle, reaching into her craft basket.

"What wonders one can do with the hair of the damned!" said Sampson, puffing on his cigar with gusto.

"Perhaps it's time to call it a night," said Miss Turner, casting a glance toward Sampson.

The strange tapping seemed to begin as if behind the walls, perhaps upstairs. Jerry concentrated, walking slowly toward the sound of the tapping, untangling the yarn cobwebs from his hands and straining to hear more. Like the doctor, his ears had been damanaged and were now ringing with gunfire. "Here?" A muffled reply from Henry. Then, another: "Absolutely not!"

Lingering, opening the front door a hair, Jerry watched Maggie wheel her veiled sister across the dark porch. Henry followed.

Maggie said, "We'll find another place."

"No," Henry said, "you won't. Not this late."

Hattie Grove said, "Why don't you ladies stay with me? I have a guest room comfortable for both Miss Usherwoods."

"You're too kind, Miss Grove," Henry said.

Sampson scoffed. "Kind," whispered Sampson to Jerry, "my ass." Jerry grimaced, not wanting to speak ill of Hattie after he had broken her heart. No man—or woman—was immune to betrayal. He only hoped Sampson would forgive him.

"Good riddance," Sampson said, tossing Jerry his coat. "Come on."

Catching a glimpse of Belle ascending the stairs, Jerry prepared to walk with Sampson, Mason, Nick, Dr. Burrows, and Henry across the lane to Henry's house.

* * *

78

Walking among the men was a leisurely pleasure because all were smokers. Once the men set foot on the lane to Henry's house, they began reaching into their coat pockets to remove pipes and cigars and cigarettes and rolling paper and pinches of aromatic tobacco. They struck matches, merrily lighting each other's cigars and cigarettes. Then, in sweet silence, they savored smoking. No words spoken, they strolled down the lane while gazing at the clear night sky and at candles burning in jack-o'-lanterns and lamps blazing in the parlor windows. The walk was too short.

Henry's house was a welcome sight for Jerry, who loved stepping through the massive doorway. The house had a charm devoid of women. Soothingly masculine as if influenced by the tradition of boatbuilding, thought Jerry, gazing at rustic walls and beams, old hand tools on display. Henry had once worked as a boatbuilder. He retired after acquiring the two boardinghouses and their stables, orchards, and farmlands. His house was a twin to his sister's, only on the outside. On the inside, the houses were in stark contrast, with Ruby's so feminine compared to Henry's unfinished pine walls and utilitarian, vernacular chairs. Henry's furnishings were plain but not stark, sturdily constructed and made of recycled materials, the pipes made of old gun barrels, retired weapons taking gas from the main.

The men went inside and Jerry watched his friends gamble. Giddy, nauseated, he sensed a change in Sampson and Mason. Poker players rarely revealed their feelings. Because Jerry now felt Belle so far above other women, and having taken Hattie from Sampson, he knew it would serve him right if Sampson took Belle from him. That night, as his friends drank whiskey, Jerry only pretended to drink.

He was sober when he heard distant screams but doubted his senses. He took it as his battle-scarred ears once again playing tricks.

Jerry ignored the sound while his friends spoke of women as if they were cattle. They placed emphasis on Aria's homely uneven face, Viv's sensuous mouth and eyes, the size and heft of each sister's bosom. Jerry was especially sensitive whenever anyone mentioned Belle.

"Cat got your tongue?" asked Nick Dalton.

"More like the sluttish sister," said Mason, scoffing into his whiskey.

Sampson lunged. The thunderous crash shook the house. Nick Dalton removed his willow prosthetic leg to prod Sampson and Mason as they threw themselves upon each other. Sampson's exposed wrist bone protruded, jagged from the botched amputation. He twisted the bone into Mason's throat. Choking, Mason wrenched until he and Sampson tumbled across rugs and hardwoods. Sampson pinned Mason and Nick beneath his long legs.

"You'll break it," Nick said, attempting to protect the detached willow prosthetic Mason clung to in desperation.

"How dare you speak of Grace," Sampson roared, beard dripping spit.

Mason moaned. "Grace? I was talking about Viv."

Nick clutched his willow leg, and Sampson released Mason and Nick.

Jerry thought he heard the scream again. He looked at Sampson, who stopped and listened.

10.

Right before discovering her ransacked room, Viv was thinking of the uninvited guests at the dumb supper. It had been years since she had seen them at Twin Oaks. They had been children then. Children! Having lost track of them, she was shocked by how they had changed. Beecher had asked her to photograph the twins at the plantation to help raise money to secure their freedom. The plan had failed. Now, she could see how the twins were profoundly altered as they attended the dumb supper with Henry Turner.

The twins disappeared months after Viv moved into the plantation. Having captured many photographic images of the girls before their parting, Viv continued posing as Mason's loving wife, working undercover to rescue the twins through the church, though she never knew what had happened to them or where they were taken. Clara Turner went out of her way to cut off all family contact with the twins, who left with her on a journey and never returned. From time to time, rumors spread that the twins had returned to Twin Oaks and were hiding in a guest wing. Then, Viv heard rumors of an unfortunate accident involving Clara Turner but no one was willing to answer questions.

Viv wondered how the twins were investigating Clara's death in Concord.

Why had the twins attended the dumb supper and yet eaten no food?

Were they with Godfrey?

What had happened to them?

Something very wrong.

Something Viv couldn't imagine and wasn't sure she wanted to. More than anything, she wanted to locate and study her old photographs of the twins. Those very images had apparently stirred such a fire of outrage at Plymouth Church that Beecher could hardly contain the congregation. By then, the twins were lost. Viv had kept some of the photographs for herself, in her box of images, to remember the girls as they were—beautiful healthy innocent children posing with dolls.

She was becoming afraid.

She sensed she wasn't alone.

She reached for the lamp. It wasn't in its place. She couldn't locate it.

She reached into the dresser drawer for a candle. She struck a match, her eyes stinging in the dancing light of the flame.

She shone candlelight around the room and found it in disarray. Someone had been here, perhaps during the party, sneaking and rummaging through her photographs and photography supplies. Who would do that? Viv's shawls, photographs, and corsets were strewn about the floor. Even the curtains were disordered. The candle could only illuminate a bit of space at a time. Moving from one corner to another, she suddenly stopped, filled with terror. Frozen. Not wanting to see what she felt was wrong. There was someone else in the room with her.

She crept. She moved the candlelight, wavering in her trembling hand. She was shaking.

When she got to the final corner, she saw what she didn't want to see.

They were there. Both of them.

Waiting for her.

Still. Silent. Patient.

Both dressed in mourning, as they had been at the dumb supper.

One in a wheelchair, face hidden in veil.

One standing, smiling at Viv.

Why were the twins here now? Posing in front of her camera, as if waiting for her to photograph them again, as she had so many times before at the plantation. But in those days, they were both healthy, lively, well. Neither needed a wheelchair. So lovely, as children, as girls, possessions, possessed.

"If you take our photograph, again, will it save us? Like you promised? Remember how you promised, Mrs. Viv?" Maggie asked.

Not knowing what to say or do, Viv stared at the twins. The twin who sat in the wheelchair and wore the black veil began slowly reaching out to Viv as if for an embrace. The other twin stood stiffly beside the wheelchair while still smiling.

The closet door swung open. Willa stumbled out of the closet, reaching out to Viv. The instant she and Viv looked at each other, they both began to scream. Viv raced into Willa's arms.

"I'm sorry. So sorry," Viv whispered while cradling Willa's face in her hands and feeling held by the warmth in Willa's gaze. "I never meant for this to happen."

"May I?" asked Willa, reaching down to stroke Viv's pregnant belly restricted beneath the corset.

Viv nodded, guiding Willa's hand over her belly, "Where's Godfrey? Have you seen him? Is he alive?"

"I have. He is. Don't worry. We're together now. He's with me now, where he wants to be."

Viv didn't know what to think. "Does he ever ask about me?"

"He asks about the child. He worries for the child."

"When can I see him?"

"Not yet."

"When?"

"When we're ready and when the child is ready."

"Where?"

"We'll both be close to you, whether you know it or not. We're watching to keep this child safe." Willa ran her hand over Viv's belly. "Don't tell anyone. Don't ever tell?"

"I won't."

Viv closed her eyes and felt the child moving inside her. When she looked into the corner of the room, she realized the twins were gone.

Another scream rang out in the boardinghouse. Willa rushed out of the room and into the dark hallway.

11.

The screams reminded Nick Dalton of the field hospital. Clutching the armrest of the sofa to regain his balance, he needed to reattach his prosthesis but froze with the loose material of his right trouser leg limp and deflated. He finally removed his pants. Grappling with straps and hooks, he heard another scream from the direction of Old Manse.

"Nick?" Henry asked, reaching the door.

"I'll catch up." Nick tugged his trousers over the prosthetic, hastily secured. He limped out of Henry's house and into the dark, hobbling. Wincing, he fell. The prosthetic, listing, angled backward, no longer moving with his body.

He limped across the moonlit lane toward the other men arriving at the gate of Miss Turner's boardinghouse. Attempting to run, Nick felt such pain he forgot fear.

Behind the boardinghouse's open door, men argued, not seeming to notice Nick's late arrival.

Henry barked commands, "Capture him. Don't let him escape."

"Who? Who?" asked Chris Datchery.

"We don't know," said Miss Turner.

"What does he look like?" asked Henry.

"Where is he?" asked Kora. "Find him."

"Did you see?" asked Sampson.

"What?" asked Nick, catching his breath, leaning against a chair.

"The intruder!" Belle screamed.

Nick was watching shadowy silhouettes of women when someone sprang, tackling him, pinning him to the floor. Hitting his head in the struggle, he remained very still and remembered the words of Aristotle: the female is a deformed male. But what did that mean, he wondered, flinching, now that he was a deformed male? Did his amputation make him female as well as male?

"Nick?" Miss Turner whispered.

He thought of Venus de Milo, armless, her ravishingly scarred face, disfigured, and wondered if some might see a sort of scarred beauty in him.

Another strangled scream, the voice now strained, chased a choked cry. Soft, wet weeping would have once inspired him to fear but, after Gettysburg, he no longer knew what the worst was.

"Nick?" Sampson whispered, helping him stand. "You alright?"

"Fine," said Nick.

"Sorry, I thought you were——"

In the dim light of a single struck match, a narrow figure approached.

"Not yet!" Grace Hayden cried.

The women attempted to dress in confusion. Except for the resourceful Kora and Miss Turner, who had wrapped themselves in curtains. Nick hoped the chaos of the house had disguised his late arrival. He adverted his eyes, attempting to preserve their modesty.

"Now," said Grace, "we're decent."

"Finally," Miss Turner said.

Nick held the lamp, shining it on everyone in the room.

Grace rushed to turn on other lamps.

In the warm glow, Nick watched the women, though hope went against his upbringing. He was raised by a prominent family in a time when, if something were wrong with a child, the doctor told the mother to "let the black stork take it." How to reconcile his feeling of being damaged, of something wrong with him, with the feeling that there was something private and dignified and heroic about suffering? Once attracted to perfect, healthy, whole women, now he fantasized about a female with an injury or physical imperfection to match his own. He felt a strange longing when he saw the Usherwood twin in the wheelchair.

Belle, Aria, and Viv huddled together, crouching in the dining room's far corner, partly hidden by the long table where Nick gazed into their faces, transformed by terror.

"What happened?" he asked.

Viv's red hair flowed down her white gown and her eyes lit with tears as she gazed at him. "In this house, someone who wasn't supposed to be here."

"Someone?"

"In the rooms, traipsing, leaning over our beds."

"We felt breathing on our eyelids," whispered Belle.

"On our mouths!"

"Did you see him?" asked Nick.

"No."

"Didn't you open your eyes?"

"It was dark," said Grace.

"I was afraid," said Belle, "if I opened my eyes, he might—"

"At first, we all thought it was one of us," said Belle.

"It sounded like a woman," said Aria.

"No," said Belle. "A man!"

"Could someone bring another lamp or candle?" Chris called.

"Maybe it was one of you? Sleepwalking?" Nick asked.

Chris was now causing a commotion, leading men upstairs in the dark, having not waited for a candle. So much like soldiers to react faster than they could think, Nick thought. He heard voices arguing. "Did you see anything?" asked Nick.

Sampson called down, "He could be right in front of us. It's too dark."

"Someone has taken all the lamps from upstairs and hidden them," said Kora.

"Could have been one of us," said Aria.

"It wasn't," said Viv, too quickly, her voice too loud.

"How do you know?" asked Nick, wondering why Viv was

acting oddly. She was defensive, as if accused, though no one had accused her of anything. What was wrong with her? What was she hiding? Strange girl, he thought, suspicious.

"I know!" said Viv.

"The breathing," said Aria.

Chris Datchery stomped into the dining room. "Nick, what the hell?"

"I'm trying to help," Nick said, but one look at Chris Datchery's face gave Nick chills—dark beard, hooked nose, moody blue deep-set eyes ready to unleash a scalding Irish temper.

"The lamps and candles," Kora called, "here, under the dining-room table."

The men began to gather the lamps and to light them.

"Help how?" Chris stared.

Nick realized it was no use to explain.

12.

Chris raced up the creaking stairs, resentment rising like bile in his throat. Snickering, he realized Nick could get more play by remaining behind with the ladies.

"Come on," Henry said. "We need to search the house from top to bottom."

"Right." Chris tried to focus on the task at hand but the look of horror on Henry's face stopped him.

"I saw something," said Henry, huffing for breath, choking on air, stumbling down the stairs, falling upon Miss Turner. "Up there!"

"Where?"

"Sister?"

"Right here, Henry," Ruby said, reaching for him.

Henry collapsed, falling onto the dining-room table. The table buckled and the ladies began to scream again. Trying not to laugh, Chris had seen Henry faint like a maiden too many times to take seriously. He thought Henry did it for dramatic effect.

"He's diabetic," Miss Turner said. "Hurry!"

Chris lifted Henry onto the fainting couch in the parlor. Ruby attempted to get Henry to sip brandy from a teacup. Kora lit a cigar, placing it upon Henry's lips so he went from teacup to cigar and began to puff in earnest, once the teacup was empty.

Chris rushed to continue the search.

"A woman," Henry called, "hiding. A woman who doesn't belong here."

Chris lit lamps and candles, giving them to the men. Running up the carpeted stairs, Chris said, "Shine light under the beds, behind curtains, inside closets, cabinets, everywhere."

"Everywhere?" asked Jerry.

"Anywhere a person could hide."

"What about me?" asked Henry.

Chris called back down the stairs to Henry. "Stay where you are, and watch over the ladies with Nick." Pausing, he added, "Ladies, look for anything that seems amiss, anything that doesn't seem right, no matter how small."

"Right," Kora shouted.

Chris worried the attic might be a problem as dark as it was. Wanting the bravest and most formidable companion, Chris chose Sampson.

"Let's go," said Sampson, holding his lantern high.

The moldy attic's rotting wood greened with damp near crates covered in black crepe. Bats fluttered from rafters. Following Sampson, Chris moved in the direction of the scattering, stunned by what he saw beneath black crepe used to cover mirrors in times of mourning. The crepe expanded as if something slight hid beneath it, slithering across the floorboards, lurking in the dark areas before crouching in the corner as it grew like a child was underneath, moving its arms.

Chris wondered if Henry had really seen a woman hiding. Or something else?

He wanted to call to Sampson on the other side of the attic but was silenced when the crepe slid back down to the floorboards. A naked woman emerged from it as if from a dark cocoon. Her nakedness covered with giant webs of human hair. Unwinding, she appeared young and slender, long black hair flowing down her shoulders. Playfully, she held the hair like a veil over her face, moving it over her body without ever revealing her features. She crouched on all fours and crawled, spiderlike, escaping through a hole in the roof.

Chris stacked a pile of crates beneath the hole. Standing on the crates, he balanced on tiptoes and stuck his head through. Breathing fresh night air, searching for the woman, he glimpsed stars, deep blue sky. In the light of the moon, he saw her on the lower peak of the roof, the black web of hair now a veil camouflaging her face where she crouched.

Chris worried she would fall. He held his breath as she approached the steepest, highest peak of the roof. She collapsed near the chimney, as if disintegrating into shadow, like a cloud of gnats, until she held no resemblance to human form. She seemed to melt into nothingness before morphing into a large bat-like creature with outspread wings. She turned towards him to reveal her cadaverous human face, glaring, and then flew away, blending into night.

Shaking, Chris stepped down from the crates. He doubted what he saw and knew better than to believe his eyes. Ever since the trauma of battle, his eyes had been playing tricks on him. He had seen mirages in the dark, suffered waking dreams. But nothing like this. Wondering what Henry had seen, he recalled the gossip about Clara Turner. She had been just a little woman like Ruby, after all. Hadn't she? And yet people said she could turn into something else during séances, materializations. He recalled the portrait of her in the paper: a little woman with long dark hair that fell past her ankles, a long wig made of many women's hair, dragging behind her like a black veil. A woman who looked like Ruby but with a shroud of glossy indigo hair. A wig, it had to be a wig. Or perhaps a Halloween disguise? Chris tried to convince himself he hadn't seen her. Besides, this woman was much too young to be Clara Turner, even if she had resembled portraits of Ruby painted long ago.

As he exited the attic, he found another odd woman, Florence Green, staring in that direction, asking, "Did you see that?"

"What?" asked Chris, thinking Miss Green different from other women.

"Did you see what I saw?"

"What do you take me for, Miss Green?"

"If you didn't see it, Mr. Datchery, how did you know what I saw?"

"I'll not answer that," Chris said, holding the attic door as

Sampson shone his lamp in corners, behind boxes.

Florence Green stared at Chris, who thought she wasn't entirely to be taken seriously, not because she was a nosy spinster but because of something else he couldn't put his finger on. As intelligent as she was, Florence was also inconstant, as if hiding something. When she blinked her bespectacled eyes, he felt guilty because he and she might have spoken plainly and honestly, comforting each other, perhaps even discovering something useful, if he had respected her more.

"There was a face, behind that crepe," said Florence. "A woman hiding, I could swear. I was afraid, too afraid to scream or to move. Then, I thought I saw her shadow moving away. But where could she have gone?"

Florence walked toward a tall pile of crepe covering something large enough to be a woman.

Part II.

1.

Ruby watched as the burning candles pooled out wax on her massive piano. She wondered if she had made a mistake by bringing Lara's daughters here. What was it like to die in a fire? Was Lara still alive when the flames consumed her? Did she ever think of Ruby, or miss her, as Ruby had missed her all these years?

Despite Father Michael's warnings, Ruby had written to Lara's daughters after Lara's death. The four sisters were homeless, penniless, without prospects. Ruby offered to shelter them in her boardinghouse, to find them good husbands. It was the least she could do, giving Lara's daughters a new lease on life.

She couldn't understand Michael's reaction. Michael was their uncle, a priest, and had helped so many strangers but wouldn't help his own flesh and blood? Unfathomable, so unlike him. He never carried grudges. Why would he blame them? Recalling Michael's warnings, Ruby was surprised that he seemed to detest his nieces. Or fear them?

He seemed to prefer them tossed out onto the streets, living in a poorhouse than in her home.

"Ruby, Ruby," he had whispered upon his nieces' arrival to Concord. "Why didn't you listen? What have you done?"

Yet the four strange women were so familiar. Though she didn't know them, they had Lara's eyes and became her last connection to Lara. Having lost Lara, Ruby still secretly felt it was her fault. She still doubted herself, wondering if Lara and Samuel Hayden would have been alive and living in Concord, if she hadn't run away on her wedding day.

The result was too horrible to imagine. No closure, all hope for forgiveness and reconciliation lost. Ruby would never be able to see Lara again or make up for mistakes of the past.

Again, the cackling. But where was it coming from? Above, she thought, but wasn't sure. She ventured upstairs but the cackling seemed to be coming from the ceiling, as if inside the attic. She lit a candle and pulled down the latch and ladder, climbing up, following the sound.

Inside the attic, she shone candlelight into dark corners and the cackling stopped. She walked to the old portrait, the one she hid away. She was surprised to find it uncovered. Staring at the portrait of her and Lara, Ruby remembered the dumb supper and wondered if a spirit had really come as an invisible guest to sit upon the throne. She thought about how it felt so odd to have lost both Clara and Lara.

Now that her sister was dead, people thought she was the imposter. She thought of Lara and Lara's daughters. Who did they think she was? In her last moments alive, Lara, whom she hadn't seen since she was a teenager, had wrongly thought she was speaking to Ruby. In truth, she had only spoken to Clara, a woman with Ruby's face who had stolen her name. Ruby's life had become a dumb supper, where she was sitting in the chair of the dead woman who pretended to be her. And yet, she used to be Clara when they were children. The game went on too long and she lost track. She had to live with the consequences. Who would believe her now? Estrangement, Ruby realized, was a kind of death, since people live on in the minds of their family and their friends.

Lara was once Ruby's best friend, her very best friend, but it was painful for Ruby to remember. The trouble started when they were teenagers, when Lara convinced Ruby to do what she didn't want to. Ruby did as Lara asked, but wondered if there wasn't a better way to find a match for Lara, who was bright and strong and healthy, despite the angry scar of proud flesh running from her forehead down her nose, dividing her face in half.

Everything changed when Samuel Hayden confessed his love for Ruby, the night before the wedding—a double wedding for the two Hayden brothers and their brides. Losing her nerve,

Ruby ran away and hid in the woods, leaving Michael Hayden alone on the altar. Lara and Samuel Hayden married nonetheless, deciding to cut Ruby out of their lives.

Samuel and Lara moved to Boston and had four daughters, whom Ruby wasn't allowed to see or write to. For decades, she had thought they were happy and well until she heard the terrible news about Lara and Samuel from Michael. By then, Lara's daughters were grown women in need of matches and a home.

Michael and Ruby had remained close to each other, despite Ruby's estrangement from Lara and Samuel. Michael became a priest and Ruby a matchmaker, running the women's boardinghouse. Michael never seemed angry with her. In fact, he only seemed more devoted, in his own quiet way. If anything, he made it clear his feelings remained unchanged. Ruby never understood why, though she was grateful he hadn't cut her off the way Lara and Samuel had done.

Ruby missed Lara, had often wondered how she and Samuel and their daughters were during the Civil War, especially when Michael reported his brother's fortune had dramatically changed. From what Ruby understood from Michael, Lara's death and the fate of Samuel, as well as what happened to their once vast fortune, was a mystery. Samuel disappeared with his family's fortune not long after Viv returned to Boston from Tennessee. Creditors had come to take Hayden House away. The family was being evicted when Lara and Samuel disappeared.

Ruby felt she had to help Lara's daughters because her twin had a part in their parents' demise.

Sometimes Ruby felt Clara was still alive. She sensed her presence. Maybe it was Clara's spirit haunting her, lingering in rooms and hallways of the boardinghouse. Lara died. Clara died. Clara has died, Ruby thought, reminding herself.

Or had she? Had Clara's face been burnt and scarred in a fire?

Clara, Lara, Clara, Lara?

One was Lara, and one was Lara with a C.

Math was simple horror. One was Clara and one was Clara minus C.

If they were the same person, Lara had never been real. She was always Clara in disguise.

2.

Florence had lost a part of herself, something few could tell by looking. When Florence was a teenager, a surgeon performed a normal ovariotomy, removing her healthy ovaries in the hope of relieving female symptoms her father thought were affecting her vision. The surgeon also threw in a complimentary clitoridectomy to prevent future complications.

Though her father said the surgeon had done her a great service, Florence wasn't so sure. She never felt as well as she did before the surgery. She lost progress, measured against other females her age. To make matters worse, her eyesight never improved. Because of this, she had decided never to marry, though she secretly desired Henry Turner.

She found it ironic that while all the recent progress with anesthesia had been a blessing to wounded soldiers, anesthesia had inspired more experimental surgeries to be performed on unsuspecting females. She wondered how many women suffered as she did, though many would have been thrilled never to worry about pregnancy.

She worried about the Usherwood twins. The sister in the wheelchair seemed to constantly hide her face beneath a veil. In Florence's experience, a young woman, unwell and hiding, usually suffered from mysterious complications because of male doctors who sought to cure her.

The world needed more female doctors. But where would they come from? Florence thought of Kora, who often said she longed to become a nurse. So caring but without the means for a proper education, Kora seemed to sense discomfort, unease, and secret physical trials of others. But Kora had no way to pursue another profession. Housekeeping was a good job, a fine and comfortable position, but when Florence thought of Kora's tender concern and knowledge of medicinal herbs, Kora's working as a house servant seemed a waste.

Florence wondered why nurturing didn't inspire more women to become doctors. Surely, a female doctor wouldn't have viewed her young body as an experimental plaything of science as a male surgeon had done.

Kora smiled at Florence in a conspiratorial manner while carrying the tea tray into Miss Turner's fashionably decorated parlor. Setting the tray down on the cherry table, she began pouring, saying, "Miss Turner, the priest will call today. Should I bring an extra cup?"

"Michael?" Ruby asked, hands shaking as she reached for her teacup.

Florence had been five years old, a flower girl among the guests at the wedding where Ruby Turner left her groom, Michael Hayden, waiting at the altar. Soon after, Michael became a priest and Ruby's best friend, Lara, left Concord after marrying Michael's younger brother, Samuel. Lara made her life in Boston, never to return to Concord. Decades later, it was still as much of a mystery as it had been when Florence was a child.

If newspapers were to be believed, Lara, Samuel, and Clara Turner were presumed dead. Authorities were uncertain what caused the fire in Clara's Boston apartment that night. After all the mysterious circumstances, with Lara and Samuel's daughters now living in Ruby's boardinghouse, Florence wanted to unravel the mystery of the past.

Florence and Ruby grew closer over time, as Ruby dealt with the loss of Lara's friendship and Florence often sought Ruby out in her teenage years, since Florence had few friends her age and no suitors. Lonely and distressed, Florence looked to Ruby for guidance, support, and companionship. She also secretly longed for a husband or some type of male companionship and she had often asked and hoped that Ruby might use her matchmaking skills to find her a suitable mate.

Florence blamed herself for being accident prone, stuttering, and cross-eyed. She walked oddly like a water bird and wore thick corrective lenses and corrective shoes. She often came to Ruby for advice on matters of the heart, on secret dreams, desires, questions about men and marriage and romantic love, wondering why no man was ever interested in her. In spite of her awkwardness and medical conditions, she was highly intelligent, sensitive, and loyal and had pretty green eyes but no man seemed to notice. She cared for Ruby's cats and canaries since she wasn't allowed to have pets in her cousin's house, where she lived, working as an unpaid nanny, cook, and maid. Secretly, Florence had unladylike vices, smoking cigars and drinking whiskey but knew better than to drink and smoke in public. She longed to gamble with the men at Henry's house but realized they would never see her as an equal. She cherished her intellect and strong, hard features, including her large, smart aristocratic nose, dark eyebrows, and thick eyelashes, yet her feelings were as soft and wispy and light as her hair, the texture of dandelion seeds.

Florence commented how good it would be to see Father Hayden, that he might enjoy a visit with his nieces.

Ruby choked on hibiscus tea.

Kora escorted the priest into Ruby's parlor.

Michael, although aged, remained one of the handsomest men in Concord with his slim form, strong jawline, vivid blue eyes, and shock-white hair.

"Has my visit caught you off guard?" Michael asked.

"You've come to see how your nieces are adjusting?" asked Ruby.

"Heavens, no. They can take care of themselves."

Florence sipped her tea, hoping they wouldn't ask her to leave, but she found it strange Father Michael showed so little concern for his nieces.

"I wasn't aware they were doing so well on their own. Before I took them in, they seemed quite lost," said Ruby.

"I worry about you, Ruby. And Henry. With your visitors."

"Why on earth?"

"There has been talk. Speculation."

"Is that all? Why don't people mind their own business?"

"Parishioners have come to me with certain concerns."

Florence worried. Though she had never known the priest to be a liar, she didn't believe he was telling the truth about the reason for his visit. He seemed beyond concerned. Maybe even afraid. But why? What might be wrong, and why was Father Michael suggesting his nieces might be endangering Ruby? Why would the Hayden sisters do anything to harm Ruby, after she had so generously invited them into her home?

The more Florence thought about it, the more she realized how little she—or anyone—knew about the Hayden sisters. Perhaps their uncle knew more than he let on? Maybe he worried about more than mere speculation? She heard muffled whispering, giggling upstairs. Apparently, the Hayden sisters preferred their own company to the company of others, holding private conversations. After suffering the loss of both parents, Florence reasoned the sisters might need time to mourn and heal. Hearing more laughter, Florence reminded herself mourning was different for everyone.

"People our age shouldn't be subjected to certain types of trouble," Father Hayden said. Sighing, he sat down on the divan as Kora poured his tea.

"What type?" Ruby, wiping spilled tea from her blouse, asked the very question Florence wanted answered. The conversation was interrupted by the Hayden sisters descending the stairs. Laughter ceased. Whispers followed footsteps down the hall below the staircase.

Father Michael stood, hurrying to the back door, saying, "Promise you'll look in on Henry? Soon."

"Of course," said Ruby.

"And look after yourself?"

"Don't you want to say hello to your nieces?"

Florence stepped toward Michael, who had already

opened the door and was stepping out onto the back porch. As he closed the door behind him, Florence thought she saw him look to where the Hayden sisters stood, waiting on the stairs. After their uncle left, the sisters returned to their rooms.

"What was that about?" Florence asked.

"I'm not sure," said Ruby, "but I want to find out."

Following Ruby across the lane, through the gate to Henry's house, Florence brightened at the possibility of seeing Henry. So rarely allowed inside his house, except when attending the occasional Spiritualist demonstration, Florence held her breath.

Ruby stepped onto Henry's porch and opened the door without knocking.

Florence tried to disguise her happiness, in case Ruby thought better of venturing inside the gamblers' den. Florence felt as if she had entered an exhibit of wayward men. She and Ruby examined every unlocked room.

All over the rugs and sofas, gamblers, in various stages of consciousness, slept. Sampson Redlaw languished in his boots, pants unbuttoned, legs propped up on the hearth. Boots elevated, head tilted back against the filthy rug, he snored, mouth wide open, beard crusted with a translucent substance.

Ruby prodded his belly with the tip of her shoe. He coughed, squinting up at Florence before feigning sleep.

"Sampson, I saw that," said Ruby. "Where's Henry?"

Sampson raised his right hand, index finger pointing in the direction of the stairs, where Jerry Rickett was sleeping. Florence paused, thinking it would be improper to step over a man. She couldn't imagine walking over a man's face.

"Don't let a drunk stop you." Ruby lifted her skirts, stepping over Jerry Rickett's head, while resting one shoe between his legs.

Florence raised her skirts to ascend the stairs, but just as she reached the dreaded moment, Jerry Rickett said, "I'm not drunk." Florence screeched and Ruby covered her mouth with her gloved hand before grabbing Florence's wrist and yanking her up the stairs. Florence lost footing, tripping over Jerry's arms.

Ruby scolded, "What's the matter? Can't keep up?"

"But Mr. Rickett—"

"Don't worry about Mr. Rickett. We need to find Henry."

Reaching the stair top and walking down a dimly lit hall, Florence realized Henry's house was twin to Ruby's house in design, built by the same architect. However, on the inside, Henry's house was different—cluttered and chaotic and full of guns. Several times, Florence tripped over half-eaten meals, plates, cutlery, broken pipes, bottles, jugs, and articles of clothing. In the air, lurked an odor of sweat—masculine sweat—mingling with urine and spilled alcohol drifting into a heavy odor like that of an animal den.

"I don't know how Kora does it, walking through this mess. I should give her an increase in her salary," said Ruby.

"Perhaps," said Florence.

When they reached Henry's room, the door was closed. Ruby tried the knob. "Locked." She knocked, calling Henry's name.

No answer.

Hearing a floorboard creaking, Florence spun around to confront Chris Datchery.

"Can I help you?" he asked.

"I need to see my brother," said Ruby.

"Perhaps another time?"

"Where's the key?"

"Miss Turner, please."

"Out of my way, Mr. Datchery." Ruby took seven steps back and Florence made herself slim, flattening against the wall. Ruby ran full tilt into the locked door, crashing into it with the weight of her body.

The door flew open. Ruby fell into the room, landing on the bed beside Henry, attempting to hide behind bed curtains, shivering, unshaven. Chris stood back, mouth agape. Florence rushed to help Ruby stand, noticing the door had opened with such force it had torn the wallpaper.

"Miss Turner?" Chris finally asked. "Are you alright?"

"Tarnation," Ruby said, brushing the dust off.

Florence followed Ruby deeper into Henry's darkened bedroom, which smelled of the grave. Behind the shadows of the bed curtains, Henry's toupee listed like a grey squirrel perched atop his fat bald head.

Ruby opened the shutters and the windows. Light flowed in and the room began to breathe.

"Well," Ruby said. "What have you got to say for yourself, shut up in a locked room?"

"Nothing," Henry said.

"What's the matter, brother?"

"Leave me."

"Henry, why?"

"Please."

"But why?"

"Valerie won't speak to me."

"Ridiculous," said Ruby, glaring at Florence. "Why waste your time on those miserable girls, when there are ladies to choose from, proper ladies like Florence?"

Florence blushed and Henry gave her a weak smile.

"Well, there's nothing I can do," said Ruby, "but we're here because Michael Hayden says there has been talk. People are saying things about the company you keep, Henry."

"What company?" asked Henry.

"Michael is concerned about visitors, probably the twins. Why do you think he's concerned?"

"Just gossip," said Henry, staring down at his hands neatly folded in his lap. "Pay it no mind, and I'll thank Michael Hayden to keep his concern to himself."

Florence left Henry's house with Ruby while wondering why Henry cared so much for Valerie Usherwood.

3.

Viv's fingertips traveled like butterflies over her belly as she attempted to calm herself.

Gazing out the boardinghouse windows, Viv tried not to think of the Usherwood twins. More than anything, she wanted to see Willa and Godfrey again, to feel safe with them but also to beg their forgiveness. Their love for each other sheltered her, in ways she was just beginning to understand. They both wanted her child to live and be safe. Now that they were in Concord, she knew they might try to protect her because of Willa's promise, but seeing Willa made her remember what had happened in Tennessee. Willa's words about Godfrey stayed with Viv, playing in her mind like a recording: he's with me, where he wants to be. Viv was beginning to realize Godfrey might not want her the way she thought he did in Tennessee, when she was married to his brother. After living in Tennessee, how strange it was to be back in Massachusetts again, but now in Concord, not Boston, living so close to the man who was once her husband.

She tried to avoid seeing the man called Henry, who had her father-in-law's face. Seeing Henry reminded her of the terrible thing Jon had done to her and to Godfrey.

Gazing into her stereoview photographs of the plantation, she remembered mosquitoes swarming the perfume of mimosa trees, Willa's dancing eyes, tobacco leaves drying in the sun, and scintillating hot oil spitting in cast-iron skillets heavy with buttermilk-battered fried chicken on Sunday mornings. Chicken in a skillet, eating secret picnics with Godfrey was foreplay when she had only two things on her mind. Fingers coated with grease smelled like love.

Viv had no idea that Godfrey and Willa were a couple.

Viv didn't realize until it was too late.

Long before Viv met Godfrey, Rev. Beecher was the most famous preacher in the country, but a pariah in the South, where people said he was in favor of the amalgamation of the races, the intermarriage of black and white. An article by Theodore Tilton claimed the mingling of black and white blood would create a more powerful nation. This stoked the old Southern fear of interracial sex deemed a crime: *miscegenation*.

She was now the most condemned sort of fallen woman. Yet it made her smile to remember Rev. Beecher's plans to send boxes of bibles and rifles, nicknamed "Beecher's Bibles," to those fighting proslavery forces. When he could find no way to send Beecher's bibles to Twin Oaks, he sent the next best thing, the perfect spy: Viv.

Viv tried not to remember when Old Jon Turner caught her and Godfrey in her bedroom. Naked as babes, holding each other in candlelight, they were fused together. They couldn't separate, even if their lives depended on it. Now she realized how selfish it was. What Old Man Turner did to them would change everything. Even he would regret it.

So long as she lived, she could never forget that moment: mouths open, tongues entwined, their bodies pressed together, pumping as if Godfrey could get any deeper into her. They kept their legs curled around each other. Squeezing him tightly with her thighs, Viv wondered why Godfrey never screamed.

Viv didn't understand why the hooded men moved her from one house to another. In the night of whispering voices, they laughed before shaving the hairs from the most intimate parts of her body.

She felt a nakedness beyond nakedness that night in Tennessee. Klansmen tied her wrists on the table. Men with faces hidden in hoods held her down by her ankles and opened her legs. She didn't know why the heated knife glinted by the light of the fire.

She didn't grasp the padlock's purpose but feared she

would be forever marred by a message she didn't understand.

When one Klansman held the padlock before her, another hooded man outraged her.

Forcing a rag into her mouth, yet another hooded man prepared to cut her surgically. After making several practice incisions, his blade sliced through her labia with precision.

The open padlock threaded her wounds.

"To keep you from any man, ever again, and to keep any child from being born," he said, securing the lock.

She slipped in and out of consciousness, listening to the crowd gathering outside the barn, as if for a celebration. Shaking and crying, in shock, she felt confused. Perhaps they did it for Mason, she thought, as a message to all wives and women tempted by what she had done.

Godfrey was not the only handsome captive.

If only she could protect him.

Viv wanted to tell Jon that Mason was in on the scheme from the beginning. They only pretended to consummate the marriage, only pretended to be in love, though no one else in the family knew.

Old Jon Turner, Mason's father, had adored her. Welcoming her as a daughter, he had bought her a camera as a wedding gift, allowing her to photograph the family and its captives, both separately and together. He had even gifted her another camera. Pleased by her hobby, he had no idea what she was really doing or why she was taking so many photographs of Valerie and Maggie.

Though they both knew the marriage was a sham, Mason had no idea about what was happening between Viv and Godfrey. Or, did he? Viv often wondered, after they were caught, partly because Mason didn't seem upset with her.

"It will be the quietest separation in the world," Mason said. "Disappear, if you like. It wouldn't be the first time a woman vanished from this place."

When Willa found her, bound and bleeding, Viv informed

Willa she was pregnant with Godfrey's child.

"The child is innocent," Willa said. "I won't have it die for what you've done."

Willa untied Viv but Viv couldn't stand until Willa used the key to unlock the padlock. Her fingers glistened, slick with blood.

Scampering, Viv dropped the padlock on the floor and dashed away, clutching herself. The next time she saw the padlock, Godfrey was wearing it on a chain like a necklace covered in blood.

4.

The sundown Ghost Gala at Hattie Grove's house advertised automatic writing punctuated by spirit trumpets. A demonstration from the Sisters of Séance, the most infamous act offered by the Usherwood Twins, promising that Maggie spoke to the dead and Valerie raised the dead while sitting veiled in her shroud. An exclusive event not for the fainthearted, the final act required payment for attendance.

The gala was rumored to answer life's most bewildering question, *what happens when we die?* Initial admission was free to all guests wearing mourning jewelry or bringing mourning wreaths. Guests were promised a viewing of spirit photographs curated by Viv, but the talk around Concord was of the private séance to be performed by Maggie and Valerie Usherwood. Taking place in Hattie's parlor right after the free events of the Ghost Gala, the private séance was for ticket holders only. It sold out immediately.

Knowing the Usherwood twins were to perform at the private séance, Ruby almost bought a ticket but thought it uncouth when she heard a corpse preserver would be involved. Henry had told her stories from men at the casket company, renting corpse preservers. They claimed water dripping from the ice-storage compartments into ice-casket pans kept a body long after death. It terrified children who imagined water dripping was the blood of the dead falling inside their houses like rain. During viewings in homes, bodies stayed iced overnight with the constant plink of dripping.

Ruby wondered how any Spiritualist event could be so cruel. Did the Sisters of Séance have to monetize suffering for the sake of mere entertainment at a time when so many houses were using corpse preservers for sad occasions?

Upon learning how quickly the private séance sold out,

Ruby began to doubt her squeamish instinct for propriety. Corpse preserver be damned! These women were trying to connect with her sister and some part of Ruby felt she deserved to be a part of that. It took less than a day for all tickets to be bought. If the tickets sold that quickly, could the private séance be as vulgar, rude, uncivilized, crude, improper, and downright impolite as Rudy imagined? She imagined the ice casket dripping as members of the séance approached a corpse in the corpse preserver and dared it to speak, taunting the dead. Perhaps vulgarity was its own commodity, she mused, and immediately regretted not purchasing a ticket.

On the day of the Ghost Gala, feeling her disappointment deepen as the minutes ticked toward evening, Ruby was grateful Florence Green decided to visit the boardinghouse.

"Ruby, the most wonderful thing has happened," said Florence, removing her careworn hat and faded gloves and plopping a suitcase on the rug. "You'll never believe it."

"What?" asked Ruby, pouring rose tea into a little cup for Florence while wondering what was inside her suitcase.

"I have tickets to the séance!"

"The private séance? You don't?"

"Two tickets!"

"But how did you manage? It has been sold out for days!"

"Please go with me?" asked Florence, her voice full of sweet desperation.

"Me?" Ruby asked, attempting to hide her delight. Like most of those grieving after the war, Ruby was trying to figure out an answer to what happened after death. Spiritualism was a welcome distraction, since she preferred to think there were spirits and ghosts all around her, not individuals rotting in the ground. "You know I don't believe in that nonsense."

"Please, Ruby?"

"Well, alright." Ruby tried not to be too hopeful of communicating with Lara and Clara. She knew Spiritualists who charged for séances often preyed on families in mourning.

Nevertheless, it was a way for women to make a living. Since mediumship was not controlled by men, neither were its profits.

"The ticket says everyone must wear black. Out of respect. Full mourning preferred," said Florence.

Ruby raced to her bedroom and quickly slipped into heavy mourning. Emerging in a long gown of black with a black veil and gloves, she was surprised to see Florence had already changed into her mourning attire and was closing her now empty suitcase after putting on jet earbobs.

Together in heavy mourning, Ruby and Florence walked around Concord while holding hands and chatting about the séance. Sundown came quickly. They hurried to Hattie Grove's property to find it crowded with a line of people waiting to enter Hattie's house to view spirit photographs, which Ruby found unclear. She saw only misty faces and shadow forms in the images. Were these ghosts? It was impossible to be certain. Where had Viv seen these things? Eventually, most of the guests were asked to leave, except those holding tickets to the séance.

During the private séance in the parlor, Maggie Usherwood announced an apparition would be coming out of the spirit cabinet and from Valerie, not only from the corpse preserver.

Without warning, a female apparition clothed in bloody veils opened the spirit cabinet doors and walked to Nick Dalton. Ruby couldn't tell if Nick was furious or terrified as he struggled with the female apparition. Throughout the struggle, he kept claiming it was no ghost but Valerie Usherwood wearing a necklace glittering like entrails.

Nick claimed that Valerie was only pretending to be crippled as part of the illusion. "She can walk," he whispered to Ruby, "as well as you or I." Nick attempted to tear off the bloody veil, and the apparition scratched at Nick's face, putting up a fight to return to the cabinet. Valerie was found minutes later, still veiled and bound to her wheelchair inside the cabinet and wearing bleeding jewelry.

"You could have killed her," Henry said to Nick after explaining mediums were vulnerable during materializations.

A music box began playing on its own. Florence whispered something strange. She claimed to have seen a black octopus-like creature emerge from Valerie's translucent veil. "I saw it climbing out of her mouth," whispered Florence. "How could she breathe with that thing inside her? I'm afraid. What if it tries to enter us?"

"Nonsense," whispered Ruby as Nick confided in her, saying he feared something about the twins endangered all.

The materialization of the "spirit" from Valerie's body took about twenty minutes once the corpse preserver was wheeled into the room by Henry and Chris Datchery. The wooden, coffin-like box contained an inner metal container holding a woman's body with ice packed around the container to chill her. But was it really a corpse inside? Ruby wondered. Perhaps someone had placed a living woman in an ice casket? Holes in the bottom of the corpse preserver allowed the melting ice to drain.

"Come closer," Maggie said, inviting the guests to approach the corpse preserver and revealing a porthole window in the lid. "This will allow you to see the face of the deceased. I encourage all who want to see her to come closer to the window. She won't mind. She isn't shy."

With a sick feeling like sinking in her chest, Ruby thought the face appeared familiar. It looked like Maggie but also somehow resembled Lara. Since Maggie was still standing beside the ice casket, Ruby was trying to figure out who the woman in the corpse preserver could be. The face inside the porthole window began to open its eyes. The woman winked at Ruby and smiled. Then, suddenly, inside the ice, she began to wail. Ruby looked around horrified, trying to see if the Hayden sisters were in attendance, for someone else to affirm what she was seeing, but none of them were there. Slowly, the lid of the corpse preserver opened.

Maggie introduced this apparition as Lara as it crawled from the corpse preserver. Lara, thought Ruby, not Lara? The woman slithered out of the ice casket and stumbled through the room as Maggie explained Valerie's spirit births left her paralyzed and that Valerie would one day birth a mystery unlike any other. Ruby suspected the woman from the corpse preserver must be Valerie and that the illusion worked because no one expected a woman in a wheelchair to walk.

As the woman approached to cradle Ruby's face with icy hands, Ruby began to worry there might be something deeply wrong. She didn't understand what exactly it was when the icy woman walked away, exiting the room.

Ruby remembered Valerie's glittering red and black necklaces.

With a flourish, Maggie opened a cabinet door to reveal Valerie tied to her wheelchair with a substance like afterbirth blooming beneath her veil. Blood and tissue exploded from the spirit cabinet, dripping off Valerie's wheelchair.

After the demonstration, Maggie attempted to clean the wheelchair. By that time, Valerie was still and silent, veiled in the wheelchair in bindings soiled by flesh, mucus, and blood.

In a room of astounded men, most of them lonely addicts shell-shocked from war, Maggie untied her sister and wiped her and her chair clean of entrails. Cotton rags soaked up blood. Valerie's dark glittering jewelry dripped. Hanging from the bloodiest necklace, a rusted padlock dangled on chain.

Maggie lifted the chain off Valerie's neck to dangle the bleeding padlock out to Ruby.

"For me? What do you want me to do with it?" asked Ruby, not wanting to get any blood on her mourning dress.

"It belongs to Viv," said Maggie.

"Should I return it to her?" asked Ruby. Searching the room for Viv and realizing Viv had gone, Ruby was about to inquire if Maggie would be so kind as to wipe the blood from the padlock.

"No," said Maggie. "Not yet. For now, I only want you to unlock it."

"But how? I don't have the key," said Ruby, still uncertain

what any of this had to do with her.

"Are you sure?"

"I only have this," Ruby said, removing the skeleton key she always wore around her neck. That key and its locks had been in her family for generations. "This key?"

"Try it, Miss Turner."

Hesitantly, Ruby eased her key into the bleeding padlock and found a perfect match.

5.

The skeleton key Ruby wore on the chain around her neck unlocked the door to the secret room as well as every other door and cabinet in the boardinghouse. Having a skeleton key was necessary in the boardinghouse, since keeping all the various keys handy was a nightmare and sometimes keys got lost. That's why Ruby wore the skeleton key and hid its twin in a place no one would ever think to look—inside a bar of soap in her washroom.

Ruby's boarders required the secret room whenever unwed mothers didn't want pregnancy to ruin their reputations. Ruby worked with Florence and Kora to protect vulnerable women, to hide them and their children, until they had a safe place to go.

As much as she found it necessary, Ruby also feared that room. Although most of the children who had been born in that room survived to enjoy long happy lives, some children died inside the room, and their mothers typically died soon after. The room was filled with shadows that played with each other. They didn't realize they were dead. Forever children. Their mothers searched for them, unable to find them. Shadow mothers weeping in the halls, their tears like rain fogged the windows. Ruby put her ear to the walls and heard the cry of the babies.

Ruby bent over the table to adjust the lamp. Something wasn't right. Her neck felt different, light. Her skeleton-key necklace was gone, just gone. Where could it be? She began to think. Where was she when she last used it? She wasn't sure. She was so accustomed to wearing the necklace for so many years that she took for granted that it would always be a part of her.

6.

Upon discovering most of her photographs of the twins had gone missing from her room in the boardinghouse, Viv thought it might be best not to look for the stolen photographs or to make a fuss. In her condition, she couldn't bear to view the photographs of the twins on the plantation anyway. It was too difficult to see the light of childhood in their faces. She touched her freckles and wondered why it was so difficult to confront a photograph.

To make matters worse, Viv worried about Grace. Could Grace be trusted? Grace knew things Belle and Aria did not. What Grace knew might make her dangerous, as she might misunderstand Viv and all she had gone through.

And how to tell Miss Turner without saying too much, without implying the wrong things, without inspiring Miss Turner to mistrust her or lead her to ask Grace about what she knew?

Well, the more Viv thought on it, the more she realized she didn't have a choice, since she now feared Grace more than she feared Miss Turner. Grace was harder to reason with, especially now that Grace didn't trust Viv.

But how to bring it up? How to start the conversation with Miss Turner? Ruby, oh Ruby, how to get her to understand? Worst of all, how to get Ruby to confide in her, to tell the truth? It was no accident Ruby and Clara looked just alike. They were not just sisters but twins. There was no other explanation, and yet Ruby never spoke of Clara. Why? Viv's mother, Lara, never spoke of Clara, either. She had only spoken of Ruby, Ruby, Ruby, and had even called Clara by that name. Ruby! So had Viv's father, Samuel. That was how the worst of the trouble started, when her father started talking to Ruby. Or no, not Ruby, but Clara. Even he doubted her at first, but later became convinced. "I was

117

so afraid this would happen," Viv had heard him whisper after Viv returned from Tennessee, "that's why I told Lara never to contact you, never to invite you here, but you're here now, finally, my love." It was enough to make one suspect they were the same person but Viv knew better, even if Grace did not. That was just the danger with Grace: that she might suspect Ruby was Clara, that she might attempt to get Viv to believe it was true. Or, worse yet, Grace likely suspected Viv was working for Clara and with the twins all along. Grace didn't understand about Godfrey or the real reason Viv could never escape what had happened at Twin Oaks. The unborn child, the secret life inside her, guided her and had nothing to do with any misplaced loyalty to Clara or the Turners. Grace, who had never given herself to any man, would never understand.

But what if it was true, what Grace had said? What if this person calling herself Ruby was really Clara Turner, their mother's murderer? No, no! That was too horrible, but just in case, Viv wanted the pistol. She wanted that pistol, she needed it. Now that Chris was making her wait for a gun, she had to use her wits to sort it all out. She had to test Miss Turner, to make sure she really was Ruby and then to test Grace, to make sure Grace knew that she—Viv—was on her side and not at all responsible for their mother's murder, not working for Clara Turner or with the twins, as Grace had accused.

What Grace thought was horrible, so horrible. How could she think that? How could Grace even begin to imagine that Viv was responsible for their mother's death? Her father's death. Or disappearance? It was so hard, so very hard to know the differentce between someone who died and someone who disappeared forever. Over time, the difference became negligible.

"You're a liar," Grace had whispered. "You're hiding something. Something terrible. It's only a matter of time before everyone knows." Viv had moved with her sisters to Ruby's house to figure out the mystery of a death, much like the Usherwood twins. Grace also wanted to figure out the secrets there.

Well, Viv was hiding something, something that others might think was terrible, but she would be damned if she would tell Grace. Grace would be the last to know. Grace would only judge her. Grace would never understand. All the steps Viv had taken to hide it—the corsets, the billowy gowns, pretending to overeat, complaining of weight gain, pretending to diet. After months of denial, weeks and weeks of no, this isn't happening.

Viv was going to have to search for the photographs of the plantation, hoping her images of Clara Turner and the twins might help to explain. She remembered the photographs she had taken in Boston after she returned from Tennessee, photographs of her mother, Lara, with a woman whom Lara called Ruby, a woman who looked like Ruby but had Clara's style—corsets and a wig of long black hair. How it had terrified Viv to see that woman and to suspect it was Clara who followed her and pretended to be her mother's friend. What would Ruby say if confronted by these images?

Maybe if Viv could find more images of Godfrey, maybe if she could just gaze upon his face, it would give her the courage to go on. If she could only gaze upon him once more and imagine his eyes, the eyes of their child. The more she thought about Godfrey's eyes, the more she thought about Willa's eyes. Soon, Willa's eyes were the only eyes Viv could imagine when she tried to remember Godfrey's face.

As Viv entered her room, she was surprised to see Belle rummaging through her closet.

"Belle, what are you doing?"

"I was going to borrow your shawl, Viv, the red one to match my skirt. I thought I could take it and bring it back before you noticed, without bothering you."

What Belle said was fine, except that she was wearing the blue skirt, not the red, and the box of photographs and glass negatives was dumped on the hardwoods, scattered, all except the images of Clara Turner, laid in a neat pile on the rocking chair.

"Belle," said Viv. "What's really going on? Don't lie to

me."

Belle sighed. "Alright, alright. I want the photographs you took of Ruby in Boston. To confront her about this whole strange act, to ask her to explain why she pretends she only just now met us, when she has known us before we came here."

"Is that all?"

"What do you mean?"

"Don't you want to know about the night Mother died?"

"I want to know about the lie Ruby has told, all along knowing we know. We get this home for our silence but I can't stand it anymore. That's why all our nerves are on edge, why she and this place are so eerie," said Belle.

"It's more than that, Belle," said Viv. "When I was living in Tennessee, Clara Turner was there. She was Mason's aunt, and she looked just like Ruby. Just like her—but with different hair and a different style."

"So you are her niece through marriage? She acts as if we are distant strangers."

"It's possible that Ruby has been telling the truth. She may not know what happened in Boston. She might not have been there. And she may know other things we don't know. If so, if we can trust her enough to tell our side of the story, to show her the evidence, these photographs." Viv paused, out of breath, and Belle, always a quick study, caught on, delighted by the plan, enough to finish Viv's sentences.

"Maybe she will trust us enough to tell us what she knows, all about Clara and our mother," said Belle.

"Yes," said Viv, "but I'm afraid it will be more difficult to get Grace to trust us—I mean, me—than to convince Miss Turner."

"We can only hope this Ruby is Ruby."

"Belle! Don't say that. You'll frighten me."

Viv placed a hand over her belly, feeling a sharp pain.

"What's wrong?" asked Belle.

The pain persisted. As much as Viv had been fearing

giving birth, she now realized how much she had been hoping to have the child, to bring it safely into the world, though she didn't know how. "Belle, I'm hurting."

"What should I do?"

"Get Kora. Or Florence. Tell them not to tell anyone. Hurry!"

The pain, a stabbing in her belly, brought her to her knees. Darkness, specks of black swirling, a deteriorating veil wavered before her eyes. She looked down, feeling as if she were falling, and braced her palms against the hardwood floor, her face hovering over a photograph. For a moment, her vision cleared and she glimpsed Godfrey in the room with Willa. Godfrey's handsome face gazed down at Viv as he and Willa cradled Viv in their arms, carrying her to the bed. Godfrey whispered, "Our child will live."

Viv took a deep breath, steeling herself, to make it through the pain.

Willa and Godfrey kissed Viv, again. "This isn't goodbye," Willa said, and Viv lost consciousness, only for a moment. When Viv opened her eyes, Willa and Godfrey were gone but Kora and Florence had entered the room.

"Viv," Kora said. "Here, let us help you."

Florence was covering Viv's forehead with a cool damp cloth. Viv focused her eyes and saw Belle staring in horror. "No," Viv said. "Not her. I don't want her here."

"Viv, Viv! Why?" Belle wept as Florence ushered her out into the hallway and closed the door.

"We're in this together," said Florence, approaching Viv on the bed as Kora held Viv's hand. "Kora and I have seen it all. We've seen it all before and have known many women in all sorts of trouble. We're secret keepers."

Viv stared at them, grateful as she closed her eyes, almost drifting off but wondering where Godfrey had gone. Kora gave her a hot tea, full of some sort of herbs that calmed her and made the pain subside. "Breathe deeply," said Kora. "In and out. Think calm, quiet thoughts. Sip the tea and breathe, just breathe."

"Kora?"

"Yes?"

"Florence?"

"Yes?"

"Can I trust you, really trust you?"

"Yes," said Kora.

"I'm just afraid to tell you," said Viv.

"You don't have to tell us anything," said Florence. "Kora and I have harbored pregnant women before."

"But that's not all—"

"I've served as midwife, often enough," said Kora, "especially in delicate situations when the woman doesn't want anyone to know. I can help you give birth, when the time comes. I can also help you hide your pregnancy."

"But I wanted—"

"Even better," said Florence. "We can help you hide your child, after it's born. We can hide it here, in the boardinghouse, as we have for many women. We can hide it, even from Ruby, if you want. And from your sisters, but it's likely best to let them all in on the secret."

"No," said Viv. "I'm not ready."

"Alright," said Florence. "We'll keep your secret, hide your pregnancy and then hide your child, until you decide what you want to do with it."

Viv wept. Kora brought her another cup of tea as Florence covered her in blankets.

"Rest, rest," Florence said.

Just as Viv closed her eyes, as if to sleep, there was a knocking at the door.

"Who is it?" called Kora.

"It's me, Belle."

"And me, Miss Turner. Let us in."

Viv put her hand over her mouth and spilled the tea on her blanket. She was shaking, uncontrollably. "Bring me the photographs," she whispered to Florence, who was watching her with a look of careful concern.

Florence began to search the room. "These?" she whispered to Viv while gathering the photographs from the chair and floorboards.

"Yes," said Viv. "Bring them here."

Kora opened the door, and Miss Turner rushed in, followed by Belle.

"I've spilled my tea," said Viv, and Kora rushed to sop up the spill with a towel while Florence stood near her, holding the photographs.

Belle rushed to Viv, pushing Kora aside. Miss Turner also approached the bed. "Viv," she asked, "is something the matter?"

Viv panicked, not knowing what to say, as Kora rushed to save her. "Miss Turner," Kora said, "I warned Viv about dieting. She never listens. She has an upset stomach, so I made her some tummy tea."

"Is that all?" asked Belle. "I thought something was really wrong. Viv, you gave me a start!"

"I'm just embarrassed about all this weight I've gained. I want to slim down, but my corsets have started to pain me."

"Happens to the best of us, dear," said Miss Turner, patting her belly, "some more than others."

"Were these the ones?" asked Florence, laying the photographs on the quilt draped over Viv.

"Yes, thank you, Miss Green," said Viv. "And, Miss Turner, now that you're here, would you mind my showing you something?"

"Not at all," said Miss Turner.

"Something I've been meaning to show you . . . and ask you about for some time."

"Well?"

"These are the photographs I took in Tennessee, at the plantation, when I was pretending to be Mason's wife," said Viv.

"Pretending?" asked Ruby.

"It's a long story, Miss Turner," said Viv, "but I want you

to look at this woman, Clara, who I think is related to you, quite closely."

Ruby adjusted her spectacles and held a photograph of Clara. Her harsh expression reminded Viv of Clara at the plantation. The same face.

Viv handed Ruby another image, this one of blurred faces, two figures standing near Clara, their faces obscured by motion. "Unfortunately, this is one of the only photographs I have of the twins that Reverend Beecher asked me to photograph. I gave many clearer photographs to Reverend Beecher. They were children then, only twelve years old. Kind, sweet, adorable girls. I kept a book of images for myself, as they were so precious. Everyone loved them."

"More's the pity," said Ruby.

"Someone—I don't know who—has come into my room and stolen photographs of Maggie and Valerie when they were young. Their entire book, gone."

"Who would have done it?" asked Ruby.

"I don't know," said Viv. "But now that they are older, they are much different. Strange, not at all like what they were as children. I wouldn't put anything past them."

"Had you seen them recently, before the dumb supper?"

"No. It had been years."

"How many years?"

"Shortly before they turned thirteen, just after I took a series of wonderfully vivid photographs of them, Clara Turner would not allow them to stay still enough for my camera to capture their faces. She took them away from the plantation and the twins never returned."

"Do you know what they are doing here, in Concord?" asked Ruby. "Twins, as you know, run in the Turner family. We have so many in our family tree. My sister, Clara, was my twin, but we parted in childhood. I rarely ever told anyone I had a twin. I can only assume Henry did the same, rarely telling anyone of his twin, our brother Jon."

"I was hoping you might be able to explain."

"To all of us," said Belle, as Aria entered the room.

"What's this?" asked Aria.

"Viv is showing Ruby photographs of Clara Turner."

"Why not show Miss Ruby the photographs of her and our mother, when she visited us in Boston?" asked Aria.

"That's what I meant," said Belle.

"Why, whatever do you mean?" asked Miss Turner. "I never visited you girls or your mother. Not in Boston. Not anywhere. I wasn't allowed. Lara said——"

"What?" asked Viv.

"Your mother and your father and I had a falling out over a private matter, before any of you were born. Your parents moved away from Concord after their wedding day, and they made it clear we would never see each other again. I was not to contact Lara or Samuel, to visit them, or you girls. Ever."

"But, Miss Turner, you did," said Aria.

Viv handed Miss Turner the photograph of her mother with the woman who had claimed to be Ruby, the woman whom their mother thought was Ruby, the one who visited so often in Boston and began to secretly befriend their father before he disappeared.

Miss Turner bumped into the table and set the lamp ajar.

"Here," said Florence, looking at Viv with alarm as she pulled the rocking chair toward Ruby and helped Ruby sit.

Ruby stared at the photographs and whispered, "How long?"

"Just before our father disappeared and until mother died," whispered Viv, recalling the reason she and her sisters sometimes said their mother had died but their father and Clara had disappeared. Like the authorities who investigated the fire and were unconvinced the bone fragments found at the scene were enough to represent three adult bodies, the sisters often disagreed about whether or not the other woman and their father had perished in the fire, though they all felt certain their mother had perished.

125

"I need to be alone, to think," Ruby said. Returning the photographs to Viv, Ruby left the room.

Later, Viv saw Ruby in the parlor staring into the glass frames where butterflies were pinned.

7.

Ruby dreaded to remember her childhood at Twin Oaks Plantation because a girl had to be careful where she lurked inside that magnificent mansion. Though magnolia trees were bountifully gleaming, nightmares hid around every corner. Marshes harbored mosquitoes in fireworks of fireflies. Dinners were divine with iced sweet tea, crispy fried chicken, mashed potatoes and gravy, fresh tomatoes and cucumbers from the gardens, fried okra, creamed corn, green beans, cornbread, handmade honeyed rolls, biscuits with butter, fresh fruit and cream, followed by dessert with all sorts of pies, cobblers, cakes, ice creams, or puddings. Along sleeping porches and screened balconies, enormous pink roses swarmed with bees. Horseflies landed on window screens. Bats wove evening sky.

Because of what she had seen as a child, she knew that women called ladies were controlling enslaved men in secret rooms when the ladies' husbands were away.

In public, no lady was bidding for men openly at auction, not in the same way men were bidding for women. Nevertheless, a wordless bidding went on as husbands' money spoke for silent wives.

Even Rev. Beecher was unconcerned. Because he couldn't imagine it, he never knew it existed. Perhaps. Or perhaps he had no interest in knowing. And, now, perhaps it had stopped, because the war was won. What had happened to them would be forgotten since slavery was now illegal and any crime that had no name could not be recorded by history. And, besides, women were supposed to be victims, not aggressors, especially behind closed doors.

Ruby remembered her childhood sneaking. She and her

twin moved through the dark like shadows. She explored the plantation at night with Clara. One night, they heard hysterical female yipping inside an isolated wing of the mansion and Ruby made the mistake of opening a door onto ladies accosting a handsome gentleman in chains. One of the women was Ruby and Clara's mother.

Ruby tried not to think of the man. He seemed a gentleman and that disturbed her most of all, even more than the look on her mother's elegantly stupefied face. What was the point of thinking of that man and why couldn't Ruby stop? Even now, as an adult, she realized there was no way for her to save violated men because they couldn't be "fallen" in the same way as women. Men like him were disgraced privately when victims of women, but fallen women were disgraced in public because they were victims of men.

She could help fallen women by hiding their pasts with a new and better way of matchmaking. It seemed a necessity after war, since the nation had suffered too many casualties. Ruby's friends were skeptical. Many were convinced the goal of matchmaking was wrong. "Marriage is a fraud of human happiness," they said. To them, most married ladies were lesser than common whores, selling themselves for profitable marriages where they were enslaved to husbands.

"Since there is a connection between marriage and slavery, a matchmaker is no better than a trader of enslaved women."

Ruby never rejected the notion of courtship because her youth had been a time of picnics and skating parties, which she tried to recapture for her boarders. On holidays, she threw chestnuting parties in the orchards and woods. Ruby remembered looking into the windows of Emerson's house, the windows of Hawthorne's Old Manse, the old gray house and Hawthorne's tower where he wrote. Thoreau died on May 6th, 1862 and Hawthorne's funeral was in 1864, but the orchard that once furnished Hawthorne's apples still bore fruit picked by courting couples.

"Prostitutes are free women, unlike wives."

There were so few interesting professions for women outside

of prostitution. Spiritualism seemed to be creating new careers for women. At first, Ruby supported the movement until she saw women mediums undressing at séances, claiming to give up power over their bodies as men examined them, intimately, claiming the body was no longer the woman's but in possession of a spirit. It all seemed a way to exploit the female body before an audience in the name of a spirit that wasn't her own.

Ruby understood why so many women wanted to become mediums. It allowed them to go into public speaking without being called sluts. To speak in the voices of dead men they allegedly channeled allowed them to be dynamic speakers. A pity, though, that so many of the first female speakers anyone paid attention to were in a trance.

Spiritualism changed many people's views of marriage because if bodies of the living could be shared by spirits of the dead, a marriage was no longer only between two people. Nor did it end in death.

8.

Kora dusted the parlor of the women's boardinghouse and the walls decorated with framed butterflies, bees, exotic insects, and birds. Kora thought of all the good married women who lived in perfect confinement like animals under glass. She wondered how many women marriage kept from flying free. No man had ever loved her the way the Michael Hayden loved Ruby. He found joy in capturing and pinning small creatures of Walden for Ruby, who knew so much about love.

When a man presented a boarder messages in flowers, Kora arranged the flowers in the parlor. An expert on the nuanced art of floriography, Miss Turner taught men to express intentions through roses and to wait for the lady's floral response.

When Chris began renovating the creaky stairs in Miss Turner's boardinghouse, Kora knew her time was running out because he had never given her flowers. Chris was a master carpenter, his labor on Miss Turner's stairs a vast improvement. Having learned the trade as a boy, he sculpted spindle rails, balconies, brackets, window caps, and dormers. Mending loose banisters was slow, precise work. Decoratively carved, the painted oak rails at Miss Turner's house had warped so the stairs cried out with every adjustment. The stairs were like broken-hearted women weeping as people walked over them.

Nevertheless, Kora suspected Chris had more on his mind than carpentry. The Hayden sisters raced up and down the winding stairs. Chris was no fool and usually didn't fall for just any woman because he thought so highly of his mother who had gone missing in the war. According to him, no woman could ever compare to his mother but Viv Hayden was different. As the stairs cried, Chris was breaking Kora's heart, even if hurting her wasn't his intention. He tipped his hat and the half-smoked cigar stashed beneath the brim rolled onto the rug as Viv bounded up the stairs.

Retrieving his cigar and sanding a banister, Chris remarked upon Viv's delicate wrists. Kora noticed his sly gaze cautiously falling to Viv's ankles as she ascended. How Viv glowed! Viv had put on more weight. Kora was tempted to tell Chris about Viv's secret, to set him right and to rid herself of a rival, but Kora wept in silence, dusting the hallstand.

Why was Kora always expecting something Chris was unwilling to give her? A daughter of immigrants, every night she sang an Irish lullaby, imagining singing to her unborn children. Like her, they would dance around the house, have dainty feet, and be courageous but fear dark birds in the chimney. They would inherit her superstitions, stories of the old country, traditions of dumb suppers and invisible guests. They would have pale powdery complexions and chocolate-colored hair. When she imagined such things, she realized it was a pity. At night, she heard the Hayden sisters settling into their beds as Kora pretended to sleep, waiting. As usual, they were lullabying in harmony as if in sisterly séance, which Kora found most suspicious.

Unlatching her window, Kora slid it open while keeping the lamp low. On the fire escape, Chris climbed the darkness of night to the gentle glow of her room.

Longing to taste the wind on his hair as he tumbled into the room, she covered his icy ears with kisses, breathing in the woodsy scent of his skin.

"Kora," he whispered, tossing off his coat and falling onto her bed.

With kisses, she undressed him and stared at his eyes before running her fingertips, slowly, over his rough knuckles and chilly cheekbones.

His nose had been broken many times and was crooked from healing. With the tip of her tongue, she traced the crescent-shaped scar beneath his left eye and allowed her nightgown to drift off her shoulders. Standing naked, she watched his eyes.

"Come here," he whispered, settling into the bed. "Under the covers, get warm with me."

Tracing his scars, she kept exploring his body with only her tongue. She begged in a soft low voice. "I would enjoy it more," she whispered, "if I were your wife." He laughed, as if it were the funniest thing she had ever said. She laughed, too, because, even as she spoke the words, she knew they were a mistake.

9.

Branches and vines battered Dr. Burrow's face as he saw Kora with Chris Datchery. Accidently, he had glimpsed them in her window while walking the night woods.

He envied even the creatures of the woods. A lone fox. An owl roosting. Squirrels scurrying along branches.

Leaves fell and he wanted to be a leaf because he had failed to be a man.

All this time, waiting and wanting a true companion, he had seen horrible things, like corpses stuffed with newspaper after being raided for organs by surgeons. He had no illusions about women, love, or his own profession.

He could still see blood-caked hands—his own hands! —probing major cavities, hacking limbs away to avoid the complication of setting fractures. The smell of blood lingered under his nails.

After the war, he followed his patients home to Concord, only to witness soldiers' venereal diseases, diseases passed on to women, and child birthing gone wrong. Sights to terrify him enough to remind him of his childhood.

As a boy, in the years of his apprenticeship to his surgeon father, he watched his mother embroider in the parlor days after her miscarriage. Suturing was needlework, his father said, though he suffered nightmares after what he and his father had done. They also studied hanged men and laboratory animals, due to the shortage of bodies legally available for dissection. Practice stitching as a young boy, he mastered the needlework of flesh. Now his patients thanked him, never knowing his medical mastery cost him his childhood.

Perhaps it was a small price to pay.

Finding a familiar footpath through the orchard, he

progressed at Henry's request, even though keeping Henry's secret was about as pleasant as extracting a tooth without ether. The sickly twins were hiding at his house and kept requesting medical treatment but never allowing the doctor to examine the one called Valerie, silent in her wheelchair and seemingly most in need of help. He wanted to excise the twins from Henry's house and all his friends' lives the way he had excised bladder stones with exceptional rapidity. Claiming to communicate with the dead, Maggie and Valerie Usherwood profited from the aggrieved, just as their mentor, Clara Turner, had done.

Maggie spoke for her sister and claimed Valerie's poor health was due to the spirits they engaged in their work. Dr. Burrows remained unconvinced. For women who supposedly communicated with the dead across space and time, they were too concerned with the body—his body.

He found the twins waiting in Henry's parlor. As usual, Maggie began to caress his face while he examined her. She was most inappropriate, attempting to distract him from approaching her sister each time he inquired about Valerie.

Today, perhaps because he had been made vulnerable by the encounter at Kora's window, Dr. Burrows felt something akin to terror as he neared Valerie in her wheelchair. He had never been frightened of a patient before. He sensed something unnatural, forcing him to explore his worst fear—death was inevitable, no matter how much skill he possessed. Was she doomed already, unable to be saved? Aristotle studied monsters to investigate undignified and indecorous aspects of nature because, once studied, a monster was no longer a monster.

What could be hidden underneath Valerie's veil?

Dr. Burrows felt sorry for Maggie. He had performed dissections of men, women, children, infants, apes, sheep, pigs, goats, and once even his own stillborn brother, yet something about Valerie fascinated him, though he was never allowed to get close to her. Maggie and Valerie seemed different from other sisters. Maggie suffered from seizures she called fits and often grew maniacal. Valerie suffered from apparent catatonia, which Maggie called a trance.

Suspecting they suffered from an infectious disorder due to poor nutrition, the doctor prepared to have the conversation again.

"Bleed me, Doctor?" Maggie asked. He thought of her veins, absorbent and exhalant vessels. Holding a stethoscope to her chest, he listened to her heart. Her face flushed, her skin warm to the touch, as if fighting infection. He thought of how painkilling became possible, usually at the cost of addiction. Fearing she might ask for strong opiates, he didn't want another addict at his door. "My sister is losing weight but never hungry."

"Not hungry, though she hasn't eaten in days?" he asked.

Maggie began stripping off her gown before slipping under a sheet so he could examine her.

"I don't understand," Dr. Burrows said. Churchgoing folks didn't expect family doctors to perform miracles but the twins weren't churchgoing folks. Maggie wanted him to examine her entire body.

Maggie said, "We only want you to care for us. Both of us. But you must heal me to heal her. Touching me, you touch us both."

Since she was speaking nonsense, he asked, somewhat maliciously, "You want me to cure your hysteria?"

"Doctor, please."

He often worried Maggie was taunting him, using him as a pawn in some sort of game. He had heard the twins speaking in a language only they understood. As identical twins, perhaps they suffered a shared delusion. Or, perhaps, they both desired him. Appearing to have no sense of boundaries with each other, they might not have developed separate, independent identities. Perhaps the twins desired the same man to remain united as they had been united by the same faces, the same body, the same birthday, and the same parents. He wondered if twinship was a sort of marriage. He suspected they took turns being each other—one day one would be in the wheelchair, still and silent, and the next day, the other would take her place.

Perhaps.

Now that he had lost his chance with Kora, he became like a man fasting in hopes of procuring the most perfect food and seeing all chance of obtaining that perfect food disappearing before his eyes. Ravenous, he was now willing to eat any food set before him, no matter how imperfect it might be.

Maggie's long dark smooth hair gleamed in window light while she smiled. Valerie sat in the wheelchair, a black veil hiding her face.

"How are you feeling?" the doctor asked.

"The same," said Maggie. "Only worse. My sister has a pain. Here, Doctor." Maggie lifted the sheet to expose her pale slender legs.

"Where?" he asked.

"Here."

Dr. Burrows allowed Maggie to guide his hand beneath the sheet.

There was something wrong.

He knew terror, true horror as he touched Maggie and the voice of his deceased father resonated beneath Valerie's veil, repeating, *Whenever I go into a house, I will go to help the sick and never with the intention of doing harm or injury.*

Maggie moved his hand in circles beneath the sheet, as his father's voice spoke beneath Valerie's veil. The father voice began to weep and moan and laugh, saying, *I will not abuse my position to indulge in sexual contacts with the bodies of women or of men, whether they be freemen or enslaved.*

He attempted to ease his own terror by hurrying to relieve Maggie with a common enough procedure. After oiling his hands, his slipped his fingers slowly inside her, a well-accepted treatment for hysteria, offering release. He was certain both twins suffered on some level, given their behavior, and that he could cure them with manual manipulation.

Whatever I see or hear, professionally or privately, which ought not to be divulged, I will keep secret and tell no one.

He thought of it as mercy until Kora opened the door.

10.

The doctor retreated hastily to the porch. Maggie threw herself over Valerie and whelled her into an isolated guest room. Flowers wilted in vases near freshly painted sea-green walls and a bed of sandalwood drapes, partly hidden in a nest of violet ruffles with lacework muted by sunlight filtered through balloon valances.

Kora hoped to steal glances beneath Valerie's black veil. Near the empty wheelchair, she sniffed the room. Dank and musty, an unwholesome stench lurked beneath the perfume of smoke and flowers. Kora prepared the washstand, gathering its jug and bowl nearer the blazing hearth fire. Walking down stairs and onto the lawn to pump water from the well, she lugged buckets to the stove to boil water. Wrapping her hands in towels, she lugged the steaming hot buckets slowly up the stairs, careful not to splash searing water on her shoes, the rugs, steps, curtains, or mahogany.

"Careful," said Kora to the twins. Out of breath, she poured the first steaming bucket into the wash jug, then went back down the stairs for another bucket of water.

When Kora had finally filled all the jugs and washbasin near the fire, Maggie extinguished the lamps and closed the curtains. With only the light of a single candle burning, finer details became lost in shadow as Maggie removed Valerie's corset, but not her veil.

"Get back!" Maggie shouted at Kora. "Turn away. She's shy." Was it only a trick of shadow, or did fingerlike marks mar Valerie's fragile twisted arms and back?

"Who did that to her?" asked Kora, addressing Maggie, instead of asking Valerie.

Maggie pointed to steam rising from the bath. In the path of the steam, moist, misty, and gray, the faint outline of a woman approached. Kora was horrified by this woman in the mist but not as horrified as she was by what she saw as Maggie helped Valerie into the water. Flesh seemed to fall from Valerie's hip. But the room was dark. So dark. Did she really see what she thought she saw?

Valerie's flesh seemed to melt and dissolve as the silhouette in the steam paused near the twins, then turned toward Kora.

11.

In fields facing the woods, Chris led Viv to the deer-shaped targets hewn of fallen trees. Using an axe, he had crafted a family of deadwood deer artfully positioned among the trees.

Trying not to be distracted by Viv's precious freckles, he demonstrated how to grip the pistol, aiming at the deer, pushing forward with the shooting hand and holding the other hand in front of the grip.

Viv said, "Let me hold it my way."

Tired of arguing, Chris fired off five rounds, just to shut her up.

"Very nice," she said.

Delving into the revolvers stashed behind hay bales, Chris had been ready to explain safety but, apparently, she felt there was no explanation needed.

"Listen," he warned. "This is your opportunity to learn from an expert."

"Who invented this?" she asked and selected a Beals Army Revolver.

He would be damned if he could bring himself to tell her he didn't know.

She went right for the targets, hitting every deer dead-on. Ready to hear any concerns she had about misfire, he was horrified she had none.

"I'm not afraid," she said, looking at the pistol in her hand. "Not anymore."

"Then, I guess I'll give you my golden rules for shooting," he said.

"Fire away, Mr. Datchery."

"Whatever you do, never point the gun at anything you're

not willing to destroy. Respect the gun. Consider all guns always loaded, even if they're not. Keep your finger off the trigger, until your sights are on the target. Be aware of the target and what's beyond the target."

"Understood, Mr. Datchery." Waving the revolver around, she unconsciously pointed it at him.

"Don't," he said.

"What?"

"That!"

"What?" She pulled the trigger and fired the gun, the bullet just missing his head. He felt it move past his hair.

"Oh, sorry! Sorry!" she said.

"I'm warning you, Viv."

"It was an accident."

"From now on, I'll stop you if I feel you're doing anything unsafe."

"How?"

"Better not find out."

"Fair enough."

"If I say stop, you have to stop what you're doing and stand still. Whatever you do, don't turn around to see what's wrong."

"Why?"

"Just trust me."

"Alright."

"I'll tap your shoulder, if I need your attention, but please don't turn around to see why."

She started laughing.

"Fire when ready!" he yelled.

As Viv prepared to take the shot, Chris stood next to her, keeping one hand on her shoulder. She wasn't frightened at all and he considered that a bad thing. He worried for her, that she would endanger herself or others by using the revolver unwisely, but he wanted to show her he was not intimidated. He knew her first experience could make or break her relationship with guns, and he was convinced she needed to know how to protect herself.

He also wanted it to be fun because she looked beautiful holding the revolver. He thought she might even be a good shooting companion, if she didn't shoot him, or someone else, by accident.

"I'm pregnant," she said.

"You're what?" he asked, thinking he misheard.

When her next shots also hit the targets, he realized she was enjoying herself far too much, especially for a woman in her condition.

12.

Ruby thought of the missing key the more she began to watch Viv. How large Viv's breasts seemed, straining corsets. Viv's belly, so round. So heavy. So pregnant. And yet Viv was pretending as if nothing were amiss, as if she weren't expecting. How could it be? But Ruby couldn't just ask.

Ruby discovered Kora and Florence whispering to Viv in Viv's room. Ruby suspected it was about Viv's pregnancy and that Viv didn't want Ruby to know, but she might have told Kora and Florence to ask for their help. Perhaps Viv had convinced them to keep her secret, and maybe Kora or Florence stole the key. No, not stole. Borrowed.

Even though it pained Ruby to imagine, she understood why Viv might want to keep the news of the pregnancy from her. After all, Ruby was a matchmaker. It was hard to find suitable husbands for women who had a child out of wedlock. Even worse, Ruby was the aunt of the man Viv had once been married to. Ruby had an awful thought. Perhaps the child was Mason's and Viv wanted to keep it from him. Well, there was nothing Ruby could do until she knew for sure. She didn't want to distress Viv. Any stress might harm the child.

Often when she walked past the secret room, she thought she heard voices whispering behind the walls, voices coming from inside the room.

She was almost certain. Almost.

That's why she didn't want to go in there. Because it might be empty.

13.

Near midnight, Aria sat in bed in the dark while listening to wind swirl against the windows. Shutters banged. Windows moaned as the hearth fire slowly died, crackling.

The house's sighs took on a pattern of pauses followed by louder creaking, then more pauses, softer creaking, until a person crept into Aria's room. A shadowy silhouette in the dark slouched like a sloth moving toward the closet.

Hunched and slow, it progressed as if drugged. The sloth, the sloth, she thought, has come for me. She had seen a sloth at a traveling zoo and she knew there were no sloths around here, not in the woods of Concord, and yet this intruder reminded her more of the sloth as it crept.

The closet door opened.

The sloth lurched in the dark while opening and closing dresser drawers. It approached Aria's bed, pausing as she closed her eyes, leaning down over her, breathing hard while shifting weight from one foot to another. Its horrid breath heated her skin. The bedroom door opened and closed.

Aria took a deep breath, sensing she was alone as footsteps faded.

A scream resounded from the hall. Aria rushed out of her bedroom and found her sisters turning on their lamps.

14.

Embarrassed for screaming at the shadow woman and fumbling to light her lamp, Grace remembered the magnificent house in Boston where her family used to live. The tinkle of silverware on bone china greeted the chime of crystal champagne flutes toasting, the crush of snow settling over the roofs in winter, and the crackle of hearth fires in the wonderful acoustics of the house built for singing. A song played in the parlor would resonate through every room, reaching a crescendo in the dancing hall. Those very acoustics allowed her to spy on her father, to overhear the conversations he had with Ruby Turner on the night before he disappeared. But no, she reasoned. It wasn't Ruby. Was it?

"After I've mortgaged the house, we'll have the money to escape," her father had whispered. "Ruby, I've already waited so long. I never wanted to live without you."

"Samuel."

"Will we go back?"

"To Concord?"

"No, love."

"But why?"

"We must disappear. Otherwise, my wife and daughters will find us."

Not long after, Aria had pulled Grace into her room. "I have something to tell you. I heard Father talking to Ruby. She told him to take our family's money—all of it—to hide it so they can escape together."

"What?" Grace asked. "When? Surely, Father would never do that. Why would he do that?"

"He loves her, not Mother. And always has. I heard, when they didn't know I was listening. Now Father is gone, and so is the money."

"But why is Ruby still here?"

"What is she doing?"

"I don't know," Grace had said, "but maybe I can get the money back so we can at least keep the house."

And now her father was gone, but Ruby was here, in her house, where she wore loose corsets while searching for the intruder. Ruby! Who wore loose corsets like that—what lady would dare?

The more fashionable a woman, Grace thought, the more likely she was to use corsets. To go un-corseted was to have no self-control. A tight corset was a moral reminder that the woman who wore it was not a loose woman. The issue was always how tightly she laced it, preferably as tight as a vice. Grace wondered about Miss Turner's corset. In the city, Miss Turner wore her corsets tight. But not anymore. What had happened to her? A woman didn't go from a tight corset to a loose corset. Not without reason.

But now Ruby, in Concord, wore her corset loosely laced.

This troubled Grace.

"Miss Turner," Grace wanted to say, "why do you seem another person now? What games are you playing?"

In Boston before Samuel disappeared, Ruby wore long gleaming black wigs and a tight girdle gave her an envious hourglass figure. Grace had been so impressed by her, but also frightened of her, without ever knowing why.

The first time Ruby visited the Hayden family in Boston, Grace's mother was so happy to see Ruby. Her mother ran into Ruby at the haberdasher's, where Ruby seemed not to recognize her. Grace was embarrassed. Her mother was crying, saying, "Please, forgive me. It was Samuel's fault."

Grace learned the best friends had become estranged due to her father.

Ruby even rented an apartment in Boston, saying it would make it easier for her to befriend Lara again without Samuel knowing. Grace thought it strange, since her family had such a large house with so many guest rooms and her mother had said

Ruby was welcome to stay any time. Then, she wondered if maybe her father didn't want Ruby there, until Aria found them together one night. She heard her father say, "Ruby, you look almost the same. I could almost bet my eyes you aren't my Ruby, not the Ruby I used to know. She was the one I banished. Not you. What's happened? What have you done to her?"

Grace shook her head, pinching her cheeks. It was no use. No use, to attempt to remember. They were gone. Gone forever—her mother and her father.

Grace was almost certain no one suspected her, except for Aria. And the twins.

She still couldn't even believe what she had done.

It seemed like a dream.

She was not a violent person.

She had killed her mother. And her father.

But it was an accident. An accident!

Circumstances had pushed her too far.

It wasn't her fault. It wasn't.

It was an accident. An accident! She didn't mean for her parents to die, only Ruby. Later, during the investigation, Grace learned the woman supposedly wasn't Ruby at all but a woman named Clara. That awful Clara Turner! Clara, the witch, pretending to be Ruby. Or was she Ruby all along? Or was Clara the one in the boardinghouse? How could Grace be sure?

So much happened leading up to the accident, the fire.

Shortly after Father disappeared, creditors informed Mother the family was to be tossed out of their home, penniless, onto the street. Mother was desperate. She wrote Viv to return home. And she ran to Ruby Turner, who convinced her Samuel was dead and the way to find out what had become of him was to speak to him beyond the veil. Grace didn't trust Ruby but could not bring herself to tell her mother about the whispers Aria had heard. She trusted Ruby. And Grace could not convince her mother otherwise.

"Why don't we write Uncle Michael for help?" Grace

had asked her mother. "He is a priest, isn't he? Surely, he can be trusted."

"I don't want him involved in the séance," said Lara. "I trust Ruby and will rely on her."

The next thing Grace knew, she was at the séance. The materialization began in the dark parlor of Ruby's rented rooms, on the rough side of Boston, near mediums for hire and bawdyhouses. Before the materialization, Ruby promised to bring forth the ghost of Grace's dead father from her spirit cabinet, but Grace was horribly offended for her mother because the ghost that emerged from the cabinet was only a naked man covered in white paint. He seemed carved in snow, but he was real enough and very much alive. He was clearly of the flesh, not of the spirit. Even worse, Grace recognized him as her father, who bore a humiliated expression, as if embarrassed to see her.

"Give us the money," Grace yelled. "Give it back. We're homeless. What have you done with it! You're no ghost."

Grace's mother began clinging to Ruby, before shaking, weeping, and crawling to Samuel.

"Grace, Grace," her mother cried when Grace rushed to scratch the paint off her father's face.

"What are you doing?" asked Ruby. "It's dangerous to confront the spirit."

"That's no ghost," said Grace, picking up a copper candlestick and whacking her father over the head, harder than she intended. Blood spurted through the white paint and Grace was overcome by a coldness as if the hand of a dead man had touched her. She suddenly realized how much fun the medium was having at the expense of her and her mother.

Grace's mother, Lara, was crying. Grace reared back, raising the candlestick high to strike Ruby, but at the very moment her mother sprang to cover Ruby's head with her body, and Grace accidently struck her mother over the head and heard a sickening bone-cracking thud. Her mother's eyes rolled back as she fell, knocking a kerosene lantern off the table, shattering glass and oil sloshing onto her and Clara. Grace watched as her mother caught fire. Her father leapt onto her and then reached out to Ruby, as if for help. Ruby tried to get away, howling in the room filling with black smoke.

Crawling along floorboards, Grace felt the others behind her, crawling through the smoke and thought they had all made it out of the burning building until she glanced back and realized she was alone. Later that week, she read the death notices in the papers. A medium and Grace's parents—all presumed dead by fire. Then, the rumors began that Clara Turner had been seen at Spiritualist demonstrations in Boston beforehand, performing séances with two twin girls, freedwomen, her protégées, powerful mediums with an ethereal exquisiteness beyond words.

Part
III.

1.

Viv knew to count 280 days, ten lunar months from the first day of her last menstrual period. She sensed the baby grew on what she ate. She drank lots of milk and rubbed butter over her chafed nipples to soften them. While imagining nourishing her child, she washed every morning with cold water to toughen the flesh of her tender freckled breasts growing heavier. Her corset wounded her swollen breasts, so she had to keep washing and covering them with gauze.

Now that her breasts and belly were getting so big, she discovered red streaks on her abdomen and thighs, her freckled skin stretching. She was getting too big, too fast. Kora and Florence had to keep helping her with adjustments to her dresses, fast yet complicated tailoring, letting out hems. She had to change to a larger corset and stop wearing a girdle, which almost broke her heart. Some days she was afraid to look into the mirror. The larger she became, the more she feared she would stay that way.

Her legs and thighs cramped. She often woke at night, suddenly, in pain. Though she looked forward to welcoming the baby, she was terrified, thinking not yet, not yet.

She wasn't ready. She didn't know what to do. Her only comfort was the feeling that Godfrey was there, protecting her, watching her from behind the walls.

She rose from bed in the dark and walked in circles, round and round her room, barefoot, until the cramps in her legs subsided. She walked quietly. Crouching over, hunched in pain, slouching as her feet shuffled, she was creeping in the dark, hunched in agony, through her sisters' rooms. Opening and closing drawers, she was searching through their things, attempting to identify objects by touch in the dark, to take her mind off the pain until it passed. She thought she was careful not to wake them, but sometimes wondered if she had. If she heard a sister wake or stir in the dark, she quietly crept away.

During her ninth month, she began to feel a lightening as the baby's head began to settle down lower, into the hollow portion of her pelvis. She felt less heaviness in her breathing and her heartbeat became more regular.

One morning, Viv had fallen asleep on her pistol and woke to laughter. Miss Turner, Kora, and Viv's sisters were delirious from lack of sleep. Suspecting it was her fault, that she might have accidentally disturbed and terrified them with her creeping all night, Viv couldn't join their spontaneous laughter. She didn't understand what was so funny. They mimicked the "silly sounds in the night," blaming a thing they called "the sloth" or "the ghost in the attic."

Was she the sloth? Viv thought of Godfrey, the twins, her torture by Klansmen, horrors of the plantation. Willa had been her only friend. She once told Willa everything, not knowing how much it had hurt her to hear it. Viv thought of Mason, her legal husband. She briefly wondered where he was and was grateful he hadn't exposed her when she took back her maiden name and began living as a single woman at the boardinghouse. Had he followed her here or was it just a coincidence that Mason was a distant relative of Miss Ruby Turner? Did Ruby know why Viv was keeping her failed marriage a secret? Marriage laws didn't make sense, having so little to do with love. Marriage was an institution, an asylum where women went to disappear.

"Our ghost," said Grace, "appears to have the voice of a woman who screams in the night."

"Funny," said Belle. "Isn't it, Viv?"

Viv clutched the pistol tighter. She regretted she hadn't told her sisters everything, but realized it was too late. They would only blame her if they knew.

"Viv," said Belle, "why are you so gloomy?"

"It's not frightening to think about in daylight. It's the opposite really," said Aria. "Isn't it?"

When Henry and the men visited that afternoon, Viv wondered if she could trust them. Before she had time to decide, her sisters began telling tales about screams in the night.

"The screaming," said Belle, "is still happening!"

"Whatever do you mean?" asked Henry.

"We heard it, again. Last night," said Ruby.

"Is that so?" asked Sampson.

"Yes," said Grace.

"Why don't you call the authorities?" asked Jerry. "I think it's time."

"I quite agree," said Nick.

Miss Turner explained, "Both to protect the Hayden sisters and to protect you, my brother, I won't involve the authorities. After the recent scandal with Clara and Lara, I'm worried for the girls' reputation and that of my boardinghouse. Can you imagine what a scandal like this would do to future business? Who would want to stay here? No more ladies."

"The Usherwood twins could stay here," said Henry.

"I feel uncertain about your friendship with the Usherwood twins."

"Surely, my friendships are not your concern, sister?" Henry asked.

"Henry?" Ruby asked. "With all my years as a matchmaker, I know when men might be playing games."

"I'm afraid there was much carrying on," said Jerry Rickett. "None of us could have heard much of anything the way it was going last night."

Chris Datchery hung his head. "Apologies," he whispered.

"Don't, Chris," said Viv. "This house seems to have gone crazy."

"More's the pity," said Sampson.

"Speak for yourself," said Grace.

"I would never doubt you," said Sampson.

"What about me, Major Redlaw?" Belle asked.

"Temporary insanity," said Nick Dalton, winking at Viv.

"Though my sisters make light of it," said Viv, "calling it

the ghost in the attic, in a few hours, it will be dark, and we shan't be laughing then."

"Just call the authorities," said Jerry Rickett.

"No," said Viv.

"Ruby's right. Think on it," said Henry. "A house full of young women traumatized by the loss of their mother and father. A scream in the night—a female scream—could have been any one of the women."

"I see," said Dr. Burrows. "So, you are diagnosing hysteria now?"

"Taking into account Halloween," said Henry. "There was talk of an intruder but no evidence, even though the house was promptly searched by several men."

"But you saw something that night?" whispered Chris to Henry.

"Hysteria would be a likely diagnosis," said Dr. Burrows.

"Thank you, doctor," said Kora, though her voice didn't sound grateful. "But Miss Turner does have evidence."

"How's this for hysterical?" asked Grace. "Most of the women in this house aren't even afraid of the screams—not anymore. We see it as a prank, don't we, ladies?"

All the women seemed to agree, except Viv.

Later that night, after the men departed, Viv was drawn to the glow beneath Kora's door. She quietly walked down the hall and knocked.

Flinging the door open, hair in tatters resembling feathers poking out from her curlers, Kora asked, "What do you want?"

Viv asked, "May I sleep here tonight?"

"And where would I sleep?" Kora asked.

"Please."

"On top of having to cook and clean for you, am I also to give up my bed and my privacy? How much do you think Miss Turner is paying me?"

"Kora, I'm sorry, but I'm frightened."

"Only one night. Just this once?"

"Understood. Thank you, Kora."

"No snoring."

Kora extinguished the lamps and Viv settled into bed beside her. Viv slept well until she was awakened by another, more frightening scream in the night.

Stumbling into Kora in the dark, Viv reached out to her sisters. Placing her hands upon their faces, she stroked Belle's fragrant cheek, kissing Aria's lips.

"Thank God," whispered Viv.

"Where's Miss Turner?" asked Kora.

"Here," said Miss Turner.

"Where's Grace?" Aria asked.

"Grace, Grace!" Viv called, feeling more responsible than she dared admit. Opening the door to Grace's room, Viv found Grace, sitting up wide-eyed on her bed.

"Grace?" asked Viv.

Grace hid under the covers. "I don't want to talk about it!"

"Alright," said Viv.

Aria and Belle embraced Grace. Even as her sisters wrapped their arms around each other, Viv retreated, realizing what happened was a warning. There was someone else creeping in the night. It wasn't just her. But it was her fault. She was convinced someone had followed her here to punish her for what she and Godfrey had done. She was afraid for the safety of her unborn. She was afraid for Godfrey. But it was her fault. She knew.

As Aria wiped away Grace's tears, Viv concocted a plan.

Shivering in the parlor, the women drank steaming tea from delicate rose china cups.

"No sleep tonight," said Viv.

"Oh, I couldn't sleep a wink," Kora said.

"Me neither," Aria agreed.

"Well, then," said Ruby, unlocking a drawer in her secretary desk to remove what appeared to be a diary. "Let's compare notes?"

"Yes," said Grace. "In my room, in my closet, after the

lamps were off, someone waited, hiding in the dark. The intruder searched my room, I think. Only his footsteps sounded like those of a child."

"Did they?" asked Ruby.

Aria began, "I heard shifting, creaking footfalls. Then, someone roaming about, opening and closing drawers. My bedroom door opened and closed. I thought he or she had gone. Then, Grace, I saw you—standing there in the dark, watching me."

"Aria, I tried to explain—" said Grace.

"Then a scream?" asked Kora.

"Who screamed?" asked Miss Turner, staring at Aria. "You?"

"No," said Aria. "I assumed it was one of you."

"Not me, not that time," said Grace. "When I woke after hearing an intruder in my room, I didn't know what to think. I was hoping it was one of you. I didn't know who it was. I couldn't see anything. It was too dark."

"Who was it?"

"Belle!"

"Not me," said Belle.

"Me either," said Viv.

"Well, don't look at me. I didn't scream," said Kora.

"And it wasn't me," said Miss Turner. "But it was definitely a female scream."

On this point, the women agreed.

Miss Turner scribbled in her diary. "None of you were the screamer?" Momentarily, adjusting her spectacles on their chain, she gazed into the eyes of all the women in the room.

They looked at her and then at each other.

"So," said Miss Turner, "we have three options, if logic is our guide. One or more of us are lying. One or more of us are mistaken. Or, the intruder is a woman."

Willa, thought Viv.

"Or women," said Aria. "If there's more than one at work."

The twins, thought Viv.

"Or perhaps, a woman and a man, or some combination?" asked Kora.

Godfrey, thought Viv. Willa and Godfrey or maybe Mason? Viv wondered. Then, a thought so horrifying occurred that it strangled her. What if the intruder was her mother or father? What if one or both of her parents were still alive and visiting them, maybe with assistance from the meddling Clara Turner?

"That would seem logical, Miss Turner," said Grace, "though I would hope none of us are liars."

"Or delusional," said Aria.

"Or delusional liars," said Belle.

"Perhaps it was just a prank," said Kora, and most of the women, except Viv and Miss Turner, appeared to agree. "Or perhaps some of us—or all of us—are suffering from hysteria?"

"Scared senseless?" asked Viv, wanting them to believe it was only their imaginations.

She cradled the pistol to her swollen breasts, rocking it as if it were a tiny child nestled against her ample bosom.

Miss Turner said, "All right, girls. Just to be safe, we'll sleep in pairs."

Everyone agreed it was a good idea, but Viv needed to make sure she could remain in Kora's room because she wanted access to the fire escape.

"Kora," asked Viv. "May I continue sleeping in your room?"

"Why not?" asked Kora.

"Grace will sleep in my room," said Miss Turner.

"Belle and I will sleep together," said Aria.

"Then, it's settled," said Miss Turner. "Off to bed, girls." Miss Turner led Grace down the hall.

Viv tried to remember Godfrey, the way he held her. If only she could let go of her longing. She would never love another man the way she had loved Godfrey, who was tortured because of her. Sneaking in the darkness, she had seen him that night, still hanging, still moving. Still alive! It seemed impossible that his neck hadn't broken, that he was still suffering, but had not died. She watched as the men were arguing by then, becoming embarrassed by the women's horror, as the women began to accuse the men of not knowing how to tie a hanging rope. Such an insult was a threat to their honor. If they couldn't even hang a man correctly, they were ignorant. All these good white southerners had botched a lynching! Eventually, because Godfrey refused to die after an hour of hanging, they cut him down.

Godfrey fell from the tree, the rope still tied to his neck as the mob stared. Viv waited for the memory to let go, then crept out of bed with the pistol.

After stealing Kora's shoes and coat, Viv opened the window and stepped out onto the icy fire escape. She slipped, shaken. Worried for the baby inside her, she dropped the pistol, which fired into the woods. Picking it up, she dusted off the snow and ran down the frosty lane, looking for a horse to steal.

She stumbled into Henry Turner's stable, the sleeping horses' breath white on cold air. Someone called her name. She turned fast, startling the horses and pointing her pistol at the voice.

"Just what do you think you're doing?" asked Kora, wrapped in blankets and wearing ill-fitting boots. "You're a shoe thief or a horse thief now? I can't keep up with your vices." Wrapping Viv into the folds of her blankets, Kora led her toward the porch of Henry Turner's house.

"I don't pretend to know," Kora said. "You won't tell, so I won't ask."

"Oh, Kora." Viv shivered violently, teeth chattering. "If I told, something bad might happen."

"Watch where you're pointing that pistol. Careful now."

"Kora, I just can't—"

"I get it. The maid can't be trusted, right? But won't you trust your sisters, or Miss Turner?"

"No."

"Gotten yourself into something awful?"

Viv didn't answer.

"Running away is only going to cause more problems."

"What else can I do?"

"You need protection." Kora reached for Viv's hand and led her closer to the porch, where Chris Datchery waited.

"I'll defend you," Chris said.

"In that case," Viv said, clutching the pistol, "stay with me."

Chris Datchery guided her back to Miss Turner's house and offered to sleep in a chair outside of Viv's room. He selected the throne from the dining-room table.

Miss Turner sat silently in the parlor with the reading lamp illuminating a black calling card clutched in her trembling hands. When Miss Turner finally glanced up at Viv, Viv knew something else had gone wrong, likely because of her.

2.

The next afternoon in the boardinghouse, a forceful knocking rattled Grace's door.

"Come in," Grace called, sitting on a vanity chair in front of her long oval mirror. The knocking on her door continued and she assumed it was one of her sisters. "Come in," Grace said, again.

Sampson opened the door, entering Grace's room unescorted. His behavior was improper, too familiar, but calling attention to it would cause problems. Pretending not to be bothered, Grace set a nailfile on the silver tray and selected an elegant tortoise-shell brush. Styling her silky curls, she watched herself in the mirror with a satisfied smile.

She watched Sampson watching her before he studied his reflection. In the mirror, his gaze moved from his head with its grizzly long tangled hair and beard to his neck to his chest, to his tattered, stained uniform, and to his amputation. He stared at the wound longer than Grace felt comfortable.

"So, that's that. It's all decided," Sampson said.

"What do you mean?" asked Grace.

"You don't want me because of this?" Sampson raised his amputation.

Grace covered her mouth with a handkerchief and shook her head, trying not to stare at his wound. Sampson stepped closer to stand behind her chair. She could smell his tobacco. She dropped the handkerchief and looked up to gaze into his dejected eyes before gazing again into the mirror, watching their reflection. As he leaned down to sniff her hair, she closed her eyes.

Just as she was about to ask him to leave, she opened her eyes and he staggered back. "I apologize, Miss Grace," he whispered. "I don't know what I was thinking." Turning to leave, he crashed into Belle. Eavesdropping in the doorway, Belle was in tears. "Don't waste your time with me, little girl," Sampson said to Belle. "Make more flowers out of dead men's hair."

"I hate you," Belle hissed at Grace after Sampson had gone. "I despise you so deeply you'll never know."

"Imagine Miss Turner's garden in spring," said Grace, not knowing what to say to Belle. She closed her eyes and tried to think of the rose garden, wanting to think of anything but what had happened.

The rose garden had frozen. Frost gathered in the orchard. Icicles formed on the naked trees and glittered sharply from eves as hearth fires warmed the boardinghouse. Windows thickened with cloudy ice and Grace sensed Belle's mood clouded with the window panes.

Grace became concerned because Belle was affected by winter, especially snow. When they lost their parents on a snowy day, Belle seemed capable of hurting herself. Belle started to gaze around Grace's room, as if searching for weapons. Belle was melodramatic, just like a spoiled child.

Belle picked up the scissors from Grace's vanity table. "I'll do it. Right here, now, in front of you. But no one is talented enough to make flowers out of my hair—flowers the way I want."

Standing before the mirror, Belle began to cut off her lovely ebony curls. She hacked her hair away, making herself strange and boyish in a matter of minutes.

"Stop, Belle. Stop! Help, someone help!" Grace screamed, but no one came as Grace watched in horror, staring as Belle slashed more of her beautiful hair away.

Belle was now much altered, her long locks gone. With bald patches like worn velvet on her tattered head, Belle held the long strands in her hands. "I'll make flowers out of my hair. Then, I can die."

"Belle, no! What have done to yourself? What have you done? Look into the mirror. Look!"

Belle paused to examine her reflection in the mirror and

howled.

Grace closed her eyes, trying to shut out the image of Belle's head, hacked and bald and ratty. There was no fixing it, not now.

"I hate myself," Belle screamed. "I'm going to hide far away. In the woods. I'm taking my hair with me. I'll make my last hair flowers where no one can see."

"Belle, wait," Grace said. "The woods are too cold. You'll catch your death."

"Good," said Belle, rushing down the stairs, clutching her hair in her hands. Grace ran after her as Belle rushed into the parlor to gather her coat. Stuffing her hair into her coat pockets, Belle dashed out of the boardinghouse and towards the woods.

Grace called after Belle.

On the lane, Chris Datchery, Nick Dalton, and Jerry Rickett were embroiled in a rowdy game. Henry Turner stood watching, safely behind the gate. Grace realized this was why no one had responded to her screams—the men were fighting amongst each other, entangled in some sort of ridiculous dispute on the lane, transformed into a makeshift boxing ring. Now they were ignoring her entirely, and Belle was likely in danger, in a hysterical state in the woods.

"Animals," Grace said. "Stop it. Stop this instant."

"Sorry, Miss Grace," said Jerry Rickett, using his boot to prod dirty snow.

Sampson chuckled, pointing to Chris' bruised eye, the lid swelling shut.

"It's Belle. I need you to help Belle. I'm worried."

"Belle?" Jerry stopped prodding Chris and Nick and turned to Grace.

"Something has happened. She's upset and ran into the woods. Alone."

"You let her?"

"I didn't have a choice."

"What was she upset about?"

She glanced toward Sampson.

163

"Why are you looking at me?" asked Sampson.

Chris rolled off Nick and stopped punching him. Nick slowly tried to stand, staggering. "What's happened?" he asked, falling back to the ground.

"Belle has chopped off all her hair and says she wants to die, but only after she makes flowers out of her hair. You won't recognize her. She ran into the woods. Alone. She's—"

Before Grace could explain any further, Jerry rushed into Henry's barn and ran back holding two pairs of ice skates.

"He'll find her," Henry said. "Jerry can skate down the frozen river faster than any man or woman can run through the woods.

3.

Belle ran through the snowy woods. Clutching strands of her butchered hair, she was praying the strands wouldn't slip through her gloves. If she looked hideous, she had made herself so. What did it matter if she would look bad in her casket? Sampson would never want her, no matter. She was shorn; no man would want her. Good. She was glad. She didn't want to live anymore. Her life was cursed. Penniless, orphaned, unloved. She just needed a bit of time—a week or so to weave flowers out of her hair while she hid in the woods, and then she could find a way to escape her life, knowing her job was done. When she reached the river, she shivered and stared into white-gray frozen waters, where a black veil and gloves caught in the ice. She wept, her body shaking in her whalebone corset. Her ribs ached. She was cold, so cold. And lonely. Even so, she didn't let her hair fall from her gloves. When the snow began to fall harder, she worried tears might freeze on her face.

Staring down the river, she heard a voice calling her name. She thought she was imagining it. Was it an angel calling, her guardian angel? The sound sometimes seemed to be coming from the river, to travel and change directions, echoing through the frozen woods.

"Bellllllle? Be-ellllle! Belle!"

Jerry Rickett whizzed by, skating along the river ice, golden curls streaming from his dark cap, long red scarf trailing. He glided as if flying along the ice, his cheeks and lips so bright and rosy from the cold as if glowing pink. Holding one hand high, he waved and sailed past. She longed for him to return. His skillful skating charmed her. Without warning, he spun around, spraying a white arc of shaved ice cut by the blades of his skates. Shaved ice jutted up from beneath the blades. Doubling back, he twirled, holding out his right hand to Belle as if he were dancing, inviting her to dance with him. Dropping her crafting basket but still clutching her hair, she shuffled in her boots, inching toward the frozen river.

Jerry skated in circles while flashing his luminous smile, his cheeks pink from the cold. Laughing, Belle realized he put on a show just for her. It was as if she was seeing him for the first time. She had never seen anyone skate so well. Every time he neared her, he cast dramatic sprays of snow through the air. The shaved ice and snow flew near her without touching her.

She giggled, such a relief after deep despair. She let go of the strands of hair she had been holding. The silky ebony curls fell, drifting down to the ivory snow near her boots.

Before she could bend over to retrieve her hair, Jerry glided toward her again and then away. Gracefully in figure eights, he circled back to stop at the edge of the river so he stood just below Belle, again bowing. "Lady," he said. She laughed, covering her mouth with gloved hands. He smiled.

"Belle," he whispered. He pointed to the snow at her boots. "Have you dropped something?"

Belle gazed down. "My hair!" Now she remembered why her head felt so strange, so cold it ached and burned, her scalp naked in the bitter wind.

Jerry whispered. "Come closer. I can't hear you."

"My hair. I cut it off."

"I thought there was something different about you," he teased. "A very unusual look. French, isn't it? How fashionable. Breathtaking!"

He reached into the satchel tied to his back and removed a pair of skates. "Care to try these? Miss Turner has lots of skates for winter parties, and they easily strap to boots. Allow me?"

"Well," said Belle, "I've never skated before."

"Never? Then, it's time to try. Let me help." He skated to her, and when he reached the edge of the river, she sat on the snow. He got down on his knees to securely attach the skates to her boots with straps.

She stood on the skates and began to lose balance, wobbling. Slipping toward the frozen river, she fell.

Jerry caught her. "Put your arms around my neck," he said, his mouth hot on her ear. His breath warmed her, making her shiver. As she clung to him, he removed his knit cap and placed it on her aching head. The soft cap soothed her, and his warm breath tickled her neck.

"Hold on," he said.

She grasped his waist and he began to skate with her. She felt the rush of the wind on her face as they raced over the frozen river. Could life be this way? One moment she wanted to die and the next moment she wanted to live forever. Her emotions filled with extremes, nothing in between despair and joy. The rush felt like a carnival ride as she cradled her arms against his muscular chest and became intoxicated by the strength of him. Placing a hand beneath his heavy coat, she felt his heart beating. She clung to him, clutching tighter to feel the muscles rippling beneath his clothing, her arms now inside his coat, her hands exploring his sweater.

He skated in slow circles, now and then gazing back to stare into her eyes. She met his gaze shyly. She let go and he spun back to face her, swiftly grabbing her wrists to keep her from falling. He grinned and began to skate faster, holding her gloved hands. "Oh," she said. "I'm getting dizzy."

He slowed. Lifting her up, holding her, he carried her farther down the frozen river by skating with her in his arms.

After they had gone past the firs, he slowed. Gently, he lowered her until her skates again touched the ice.

"I'm slipping," she said. Grabbing her hands, pulling her against him, steadying her, he moved his face toward hers. They kissed. Small dark birds flew from naked elms as their lips parted. She closed her eyes, leaning into him to feel his heart racing. His tongue flitted over her lips and they breathed into each other. It was her first real kiss.

He grinned so the lines around his blue eyes crinkled.

Reaching down, he tore off a loose thread from his coat and wrapped the thread around her gloved engagement finger, tying it there. "With this string, I thee wed," he said, pulling her close and kissing her face, again, in short soft kisses.

She wrapped her arms around him, and heard voices echoing through the woods. "Jerry, Jerry! Belle?" the voices called.

"Here," Jerry called out. "Over here."

Belle's heart sank. She didn't want their privacy to be interrupted, to share him with anyone else, or to be separated from him ever again. He held her gloved hands, then straightened the string wrapped around her finger, before giving her a wink. She stared down at the thread, thin but strong, tightly knotted. She wondered if he was serious when he asked her, if he really planned on marrying her or was only teasing. She laughed.

Far down the river, skaters in pairs approached. Sampson and Grace led the way, followed by Chris and Viv. They skated toward Jerry and Belle.

Belle wobbled.

"Come here," Jerry said to Belle. "You're alright. Hold me tight."

She wrapped her arms around his neck and he lifted her off the ice. Cradling her, one arm behind her neck and one arm under her knees, he skated while carrying her, before setting her skates on the ice and waiting for her to rebalance as he held her hands, so he could guide her gently.

As a group of three pairs, Sampson and Grace, Chris and Viv, and Jerry and Belle followed the river back, skating toward Ruby Turner's boardinghouse. The evening sky darkened above them. Inside the boardinghouse that night, they warmed their hands by the hearth fire and found Aria playing piano for Nick Dalton. Nick and Aria were singing in unexpectedly tender harmony.

A dinner of chicken sandwiches had been prepared by Kora. While Aria played piano, everyone else ate standing before the blazing hearth. Belle stood next to the fire, feeling the warmth of its flames and of Jerry's arms around her, his face nuzzling the crook of her neck. Shivering in warmth, she listened to Aria's new song and had never heard any song like it before. Aria had been crafting the melody, weaving chords day and night.

"Won't you eat?" Belle asked Aria.

"No, I want to finish my song. It's close. So close. Somewhere in here," Aria said, tapping the keys as Jerry let go of Belle.

When Belle turned around, Jerry had gone.

"Where's Jerry?" Belle asked, her heart sinking, sorry she had given him a chance to slip away.

"No idea," said Sampson.

"Gone," said Chris. "He'll probably be back soon."

"Where did he go?"

"Didn't say."

More than an hour later, Jerry finally returned, shivering, covered in snow.

Belle ran to him, throwing her arms around him before she led him to the fire to warm him. By the amber light of the flames, he reached into his coat pocket to retrieve her shorn hair gleaming in his hands.

Belle gazed longingly into Jerry's eyes and wondered how much longer they could keep their engagement a secret.

4.

While the couples courted and sang near the piano, Ruby traced the scratches scrawled on black paper calling cards: Clara Turner. She laughed, realizing someone might be playing a prank on her. Was it meant to imply Clara had been the invisible guest at the dumb supper?

Running her fingertips over the scrawls, the deep, heavy scratches, Ruby could not make herself believe they were written by a dead woman. These were angry scratches, deep and ragged, full of rage. But who would care enough, or know enough, about Clara to have carved her signature?

Later that night while sitting at the desk in her bedroom, Ruby discovered a black envelope. She opened it with care. Inside, she found a letter written in blood. It read:

Dear Ruby,

To show there are no hard feelings, I will gift all the ladies in your boardinghouse with necklaces of blood in the night, making them beautiful like me.

Love Always,
Your Sister

Fearing she and her boarders were in danger, recalling the blood jewelry Valerie Usherwood wore at the private séance in Hattie's house, Ruby sent Chris Datchery to fetch Michael Hayden so that the three could meet in her library. She wanted Michael's advice, since he was the wisest person she knew and her oldest friend, but first, before she showed Michael the blood letter, she needed him to understand what had happened at Hattie Grove's house. She asked Chris to describe the blood jewelry at the Ghost Gala.

"I've heard enough," said Michael as Chris attempted to describe the blood jewelry by comparing it to field-hospital floors during amputations and surgeries for gunshot wounds to the stomach, "perhaps the twins will soon leave, if we convince them to make other arrangements."

"Such as?" asked Ruby.

"I doubt they could afford a hotel," said Chris.

"Seems," said Father Hayden. "But who would put them up?"

Chris said, "Henry."

"The fool," Ruby whispered, thinking how improper it was. Mediums rarely worried about propriety. Ruby supposed the only reason they hadn't moved into Henry's house right away was because the place was filthy, foul, and crowded with men gambling all night. Or, perhaps, the twins had other reasons. Perhaps they didn't like being chased or having to perform all day and all night, being looked at as sensations, rather than as people.

"They're not worth the risk," said Michael, "with spirits of the lower astral plane deceiving the living by impersonating the dead."

"You don't actually believe the twins contact spirits?" asked Ruby.

"Our thoughts are written in invisible ink," said Michael. "Some people use spirits to see and hear and feel what is written in astral light. If the twins can read this invisible ink, like God, I doubt their ability to correctly interpret such messages, or even discern their source."

"Agreed," said Ruby.

"Responsible occultists—if there is such a thing— recognize not all discarnate entities are of human evolution," said Michael. "I don't support any séances, but if one must attend such gatherings, mediums should take precautions by recognizing the lowest of the chain of beings is subhuman."

"Michael?" whispered Ruby. A handkerchief pressed to her lips, she began to wonder if her recent dumb supper had been a mistake. She wondered if the intruder was not human but something subhuman entering her home, something she accidently invited that needed to be evicted. Then, she began to laugh at how ridiculous it seemed.

"What's so funny?" asked Chris.

"It's easy for them to impersonate the departed," said Michael.

"Why?" asked Chris.

"Because death has made spirits naked, unrecognizable even to their loved ones, since they are no longer clothed in flesh," said Michael.

"A horrible sort of nakedness," said Ruby, shivering to recall the rumors about séances where the twins birthed naked, sweaty creatures speaking in blood. Ruby reached out to Michael. "What about the invisible guest I invited to the dumb supper? Nothing could have actually come to sit in the empty throne?"

5.

Viv, Grace, Aria, and Belle left the house, holding skates. Ruby was grateful to Florence for inviting the girls for tea before organizing an ice-skating outing with the men. Belle, who had recently learned to ice skate, had taken to it so, and Grace was already such a fine skater. All the men skated, except for Nick, who would likely stay with Aria and Florence at Florence's piano, singing harmony. This little outing was just what the girls needed after the screams in the night. It was also just what Ruby needed to get the girls out of the boardinghouse so she could search every room without alarming them.

After the Hayden sisters left for Florence's tea, Kora assured Ruby that she knew the boarders' hiding places, where women often stashed intimate items. Ruby told Kora that she would look in those places, but she really wanted to find evidence of something else. She wanted to discover if someone was hiding in the boardinghouse and where that person might be hiding.

"If that's the case," said Kora, "we need to ask someone who knows how to hide."

"Like who?"

"Chris will know. Any of the soldiers might."

"Yes, but he's already getting ready to skate. Isn't he?"

"He won't want to if Viv isn't skating, and she's in no condition to skate today, is she? Besides, Chris wants to protect her from whatever has been happening here. He'll help us, if we ask."

"Good. Go ask him. Hurry! And, Kora?" Ruby said, since something had just occurred to her. She recalled all the many times in Sampson's youth when she caught him hiding in her boardinghouse to spy on the women. Even as a teenager, Sampson had assured her that he knew places to hide in her boardinghouse that even Ruby would never guess.

"Yes?" asked Kora.

"Bring Sampson along as well, won't you? Tell him we need a special favor."

"Very well, Miss. But he'll be sorry not to skate with the girls."

"Tell him it's for me."

"I will."

Not more than half an hour later, Kora returned to the boardinghouse with Sampson and Chris.

"At your service, Miss Turner," Sampson said to Ruby. "What's all this about?"

"I need you to show me all the hiding places here. You used to know them?"

"Certainly. You still think you have an uninvited guest?"

"I do." Ruby promptly showed Sampson the blood letter. Sampson showed the letter to Chris, who showed it to Kora, and the four of them began searching house thoroughly, starting with the boarders' rooms.

Belle's room was a mess of crafting supplies, nests of human hair partly woven into flowers. Aria's room was neat and Viv's room smelled of photographic chemicals, her large cameras taking up most of the floor space, her closet used as a darkroom, so her dresses wilted on chairs.

"See," said Kora in Grace's room with its lovely vanity mirror and the desk with locked drawers.

Chris knelt beside the desk, taking a few small metal tools from his pockets. With a tiny knife, he forced the lock, and the drawers popped open.

"Stand back," Sampson said, plunging his hand into a drawer of heavily perfumed corsets, girdles, and garters.

"Sampson!" Ruby scolded.

Sampson pulled the desk away from the wall, discovered nothing but dust. He searched under the bed, pulling back the ruffled skirt to reveal shadowed flooring.

Then, he opened the closet door and pushed back robes,

174

coats, and gowns on their hangers, before stooping to examine the closet floor. He seemed not to notice the camouflaged door to the secret room.

"Chris," Sampson said, "look here."

Ruby peered into the closet where Sampson pointed. Beneath the shadow of Grace's gowns, velvet blankets were bunched in a distinctive shape, as if someone had been sitting on the blankets for a long time, the imprint clearly visible. Ruby wondered how long someone would have to sit there in the closet to make such an imprint.

"Who has been hiding in Grace's closet?" asked Kora.

"And why?" asked Chris.

"Allow me to hide in Grace's closet tonight," said Sampson, "I'll see if I can spring on the person who has been sneaking."

Though she reluctantly agreed, Ruby was pleased to have Sampson hiding in the boardinghouse and thought Sampson's idea was their best hope.

6.

Listening to Grace snore while standing in the closet with her shawls and gowns, Sampson felt drunk on perfume and fought to stay awake. Ostrich shawl feathers tickled his nose. Suppressing a sneeze, he sweated as if ants were walking over his forehead.

Knocking a hatbox off its shelf, he heard a clatter on the other side of the closet door. His heart skipped a beat. Crouching in the dark, holding his breath, he sensed Grace moving.

"Who's there?" Grace asked.

Sampson held his breath.

The closet door opened.

She sprang, clawing at his face and neck. He put his hand over her mouth to stop her from screaming. "It's me. Sampson."

If he could have reached the lamp, he might have been able to talk sense and convince her he was not the intruder. He needed light because the more he tried to explain his situation, the less sense it made. He realized no matter what he said, she would think he was the intruder.

Grace had not asked for his protection, so he had, in a sense, forced himself upon her. "I'm sorry," he said, realizing he had violated her privacy.

She struck his face, stinging him with slaps. He tasted blood. It was the most vicious attack he had ever encountered from any woman.

"Grace," he said, shielding his eyes with his left arm, but he didn't dare fight or defend himself because he knew he was in the wrong. Could he find a way to prove himself to her?

"Grace," he whispered, ducking again. "Please, stop."

He removed his hand from her mouth.

Grace slapped him, again, bringing more blood, but whispering his name. This was how he knew she realized she wasn't in any real danger.

"Sampson?" she asked.

"I didn't mean to frighten you," he whispered.

"Let go," she said, pulling away.

She turned on the lamp, shining it in his eyes.

"You're bleeding," she said.

He wiped the blood on his sleeve.

She craned her neck, her gaze jolting up to the ceiling. "What was that?"

"What?"

Footsteps on the ceiling, rapidly pattering and creaking, leapt in what must have been an attic storage space directly above Grace's room.

"That!" Grace tied her robe tightly around her waist and Sampson followed her into the dark attic.

Debris fell, raining down. Grace coughed. What caught in her hair reeked of decay, something rotten retreating into earth. Footsteps creaked and the weary bones of the house groaned. Grace remained calm until she heard breathing behind her.

Sampson stood directly in front of her. She held his hand in one hand and a candle in the other. When she finally realized someone was behind her in the darkness, she let go of Sampson's hand. The candle went out. Grace swung around, lashing out at the air behind her.

She scraped support beams, breaking her fingernails, splinters cutting her fingertips. She growled. Her feet, bare, stepped on what felt like lint or delicate clothing, so soft, disintegrating beneath satin gowns, powdery corsets wilting like corsages of old lace.

Weaving between cobwebs and rafters, she found the

back wall of the attic and touched a body. She tugged long hair. "Who are you? Where are your clothes?" she whispered. Her fingers trailed down, traveling a sunken silken belly.

"Sampson," Grace said. Hearing laughter behind her, she froze.

"Grace?" Sampson asked, his voice coming from the other side of the attic. "Are you laughing?"

"I'm not," Grace said.

"I thought I heard you."

"That's not me."

The laughter, again, crazed, womanly, resounded throughout the darkness behind Grace. She heard a crash, tussling across floorboards, and a thud. Crates toppled, splintering apart, spilling their contents.

The naked woman grasped Grace's hands and began to run Grace's hands up and down her body. The woman felt so cold to the touch that Grace feared the woman was dead. The woman's body felt as if she had been stored in ice. What if she was a prisoner? What if she was one of Grace's sisters and something had happened to her so that she wouldn't or couldn't speak? What if she was wounded, bound, unconscious? Grace reached up to touch the woman's face. The woman lurched with harsh, ragged breathing and ran toward Sampson. Grace heard a crash followed by a groan.

"I've caught our intruder," said Sampson. "A woman much indisposed."

With a length of cord, Grace tied the woman's wrists. The woman did not fight but allowed herself to be bound. Grace looped the cord around the woman's neck like a leash and offered the leash to Sampson, who removed his coat and draped it over the woman's shoulders.

Grace opened the attic hatch. Dim light fell, too dim for Grace to recognize the woman's face.

"She doesn't move," said Grace. "Pull her."

"No," said Sampson.

Grace remembered smooth hands, so cold, beneath her gown.

She walked down the attic ladder. Her aching eyes adjusted to the lamplight as she reached for the kerosene lantern on the table and shone it on the attic hatch.

Sampson whispered, "Take care not to fall."

But the naked woman was already falling through the attic hatch, dangling from her leashed wrists like a puppet, hanging. Grace gasped, suppressing a scream.

A slim white foot shimmered translucent, revealing blue-violent veins. Smooth white hairless legs, a shapely waist, and small delicate breasts hung beneath a swanlike neck supporting an exquisite face with glassy eyes. Maggie Usherwood choked as she said, "My sister..."

Sampson stared straight ahead, never glancing at Maggie. As he adjusted his coat to cover her nakedness, he struggled to preserve Maggie's dignity and his own, though his face matched the color of his ginger beard.

"Careful," Grace whispered so as not to wake the house.

Wrapping his coat around Maggie, again, Sampson hoisted her over his shoulder like a sack of grain. Grace wondered if both twins were mentally disturbed or physically unwell. It was hard to know whether to care for them or imprison them, whether to pity them or to shun them.

She realized she would have to do both.

With Maggie slung over his shoulder, Sampson entered Grace's room just before Grace closed the door.

After placing Maggie on the bed, Sampson tore the curtains off the windows and tossed them over her.

Grace arranged the curtains over Maggie, who refused to answer any questions.

Grace kept asking:

"What were you doing?"

"Where are your clothes?"

"Was that you in my bedroom?"

"What do you want with Miss Turner? Or, is it me and my sisters you're after?"

"Why are you here?"

"Is this some sort of game?"

Maggie turned away, staring at the mirror with blank eyes. Sampson tied Maggie's wrists and ankles to the bedposts.

"We're getting nowhere," said Sampson. "Can you watch her while I go for help?"

"Will you find her twin?" asked Grace.

"No," said Maggie, seeming to contradict her earlier request. "You find her, Miss Grace."

Sampson stomped out of the room leaving Grace to stare at the curtains slipping from Maggie's bound arms. Maggie seemed so calm at times and, at other times, as if she were laughing at some private joke. She was a woman, Grace realized, who had been bound many times before, even chained.

Almost an hour later, Grace heard scuffing and male voices bickering quietly. Grace opened the door and saw the men carrying Valerie's chair up the stairs. Viv, Belle, and Aria peeked their heads out of their rooms, as Sampson and his friends lugged Valerie and her wheelchair.

Once Valerie was placed inside the room, Grace asked the men to leave so she could be alone with the twins, since Maggie was still indisposed, but Sampson insisted he would stay to protect Grace.

After all the men except Sampson left, Grace sensed something between the silent sisters, as if Valerie communicated with Maggie in a wordless language, covered in her veil and gloves and long, black gossamer. Grace reasoned it was necessary for the sisters to communicate discretely due to their calling.

Maggie finally said, "Leave my sister alone."

Grace backed away from Valerie, fearing the twins

had long ago constructed a secret language to thrive in silence. Grace imagined it began in infancy. For as long as Grace remembered, she and her sisters had kept secrets, not secrets for each other, but from each other.

Maggie seemed to echo Grace's thoughts, smiling weirdly and saying, "We knew how to conspire, even in the cradle. We were silent for so long after our birth that our captors almost gave us up, thinking we were slow, dimwitted, damaged darlings."

Grace started to feel pity for them until Maggie frightened her by saying, "We were never what Clara Turner thought we were."

"What do you mean?" asked Grace.

"Silence was what first allowed us to hear what others could not."

"Such as?"

"We never spoke to anyone but each other, until Clara Turner became aware of our gifts and knew ours were in line with hers. People came to see what we could do."

Grace and Sampson stared at Maggie.

Maggie rocked in her bindings, shifting in curtains. Valerie, unmoving, her face still veiled, held still as Maggie wriggled wormlike.

"Mr. Redlaw," Maggie whispered in her sweetest voice, "do you trust Grace?"

Grace also heard a very soft, almost inaudible but nonsensical, childlike raving, scathing, coming from beneath Valerie's veil.

Sampson seemed not to hear it.

Grace checked Maggie's bindings beneath the curtains. Steeling herself, Grace wondered what the twins actually knew and if anyone would believe them.

"Can't you see what she's doing, Mr. Redlaw?" asked Maggie. "Please, let us go."

"Why the attic?" Sampson asked.

"To keep track of Grace," said Maggie, "and to make use of the corpse preserver stored up there."

That's when Grace thought she heard Valerie, in the silent voice saying, *stupid, stupid girl*. Sampson seemed not to hear it, just like last time, and Maggie gave Grace a wink.

"You're innocent victims?" asked Sampson, fingers working his matted beard. "And Grace is the deviant?"

Bandages unraveled from his botched amputation where bone jutted through wrappings frayed. Grace realized he had endured great pain and considered him hardened while wondering if he would care if something happened to the twins.

Maggie asked, "Will you let us go or give us a place to hide?"

"What do you think?" asked Grace.

"You already know too much," said Maggie, and Grace thought she heard Valerie's voice, again: *enough to ruin us*.

"Everyone must be sworn to secrecy," Maggie said.

Some secrets should never be told.

"Why?" Sampson asked and then gazed at Grace.

Maggie interrupted. "We're working for someone we fear."

"Who?" asked Grace.

"Someone who hates you," said Maggie. "And your sisters."

"Who?" asked Grace, again.

"Think," Sampson said.

"Yes?" asked Maggie.

Sister?

Sampson whispered in Grace's ear before leaving the room, "Careful."

Fearing the twins knew her secret about the Boston fire, Grace turned toward Valerie, her face still covered in the mourning veil. The veil began to move as if stirred by wind as a deep, grating laughter emanated from Valerie. The laughter seemed to move inside Grace. She felt it vibrating inside her chest, and the next thing she knew, she was laughing in a voice that wasn't her own, even though she didn't want to laugh and had no idea what was funny.

The curtains rustled as Maggie attempted various manual gestures with bound hands. As her fingers moved, Grace's body began to move in response, as if Grace were a marionette on sensitive string.

"Don't you look for answers you don't want to find. And don't you ever, ever try to separate me from my sister," hissed Maggie.

Grace, who often argued with her sisters, thought separation was the thing the twins hated most because the door to one mind closed to the other. Like being alone in a windowless room in the dark.

A violent rapping and crashing ricochet reverberated as if behind the walls. Maggie cracked the joints of her fingers and toes. Stealthy entreaties, begging for reconciliation, or a warning of what was to come?

Maggie cried like a little child lost in the woods.

Grace approached the wheelchair, ready to finally tear off Valerie's veil. She had to see what Valerie was hiding and why. Stepping closer to Valerie in her chair, Grace reached out to the veil just as Henry Turner burst through the bedroom door. Shoving Grace aside, he rushed to Valerie and held her veiled head in his hands. Grace, hearing a slight crunch, worried Henry would crack Valerie's skull like a nut.

Maggie wept.

"Thank god," Henry said to Maggie while stroking Valerie's veil, tenderly, gently.

Maggie jerked her chin down to where she was bound beneath curtains on Grace's lumpy mattress, bedsprings screeching.

"Tied?" Henry asked.

"A necessary precaution," said Grace.

Henry asked, "Where are her clothes?"

"Good question," said Grace. "I would love to hear the answer."

"What do you mean?" asked Henry.

"Does the veiled sister ever talk?"

Maggie stared with what appeared to be traumatized eyes.

Henry said, "My precious, don't worry."

Grace suspected his pockets were as deep as his heart, a bad combination with a shallow mind. Infatuation made him an easy target.

Ruby entered with a flourish of her velvet robe. Grace had never been so happy to see her.

"Miss Ruby Turner," said Maggie. "Just the person I wanted to see."

Grace wondered why Maggie was so pleased to see Ruby, who seemed to be ignoring the twins and speaking to Henry.

"Remember," Grace thought she heard Henry whisper to Ruby, "when Mother died?"

"Henry," Maggie said, weeping. "There's been a misunderstanding. Please!"

"Don't worry, pet," he said, placing his fatty palms on either side of Valerie's veiled head to press her ears. He grasped her head tenderly. "I'm here," he whispered, though Valerie never responded to him, never lifted her head.

Finally releasing Valerie, Henry turned to Grace and said, "Put your dog on a chain."

"I don't have a dog," said Grace.

"Of course, you do. His name is Sampson!"

"Well, I never," said Grace, her gaze moving to the mirror, her reflection resembling a haughty queen before beheading. If she could control Sampson as if he were a dog, a powerful faithful beast at her command, what a dangerous pair they would make. Maggie seemed to mistake Grace's trembling as a sign of weakness.

Grace was about to address Maggie, to try to communicate with her, woman to woman, to find out what she knew, about Clara or Ruby or that night when Grace was caught in the fire, but just as she was about to open her mouth, she heard a knock at the door.

Jerry Rickett and Nick Dalton entered the room. Grace was struck by Jerry's classic features. By comparison, Sampson was like a caveman with his filthy uncombed beard, the matted tangled hair falling into his eyes. Grace was grateful that Sampson had not taken the twins' warning seriously. What would happen if the twins started telling everyone she was a murderer?

"What's this game?" Nick asked.

"Does it look like a game?" asked Grace.

"Yes," said Nick.

"Sampson and Miss Grace behaved terribly," said Henry.

Sampson gave Grace a look. It disturbed her and still somehow filled her with longing.

"I've been brutalized," said Grace. "I would rather not say how. That would be more brutality."

"My dear," said Henry. "We never would have guessed."

"What does that mean, Mr. Turner?" asked Grace.

Sampson stared at Grace.

"Do explain," said Jerry.

Henry, again attempting to defend Maggie and Valerie, seemed about to untie Maggie. Grace stopped him, telling what had occurred in her room and in the attic.

"Incredible," Jerry said. "You think it was them?"

"They're frauds, criminals, who have violated this house and my privacy. God knows what else they've done!" said Grace.

We're not frauds.

Maggie said, "We're true Spiritualists. Mediums. We help people communicate with the dead."

"I never doubted it," said Henry.

"We are conduits," said Maggie. "My sister is the vessel. I'm the voice. But we're not the intruder. The intruder is the spirits we're attempting to communicate with—one who follows Ruby and Grace, one who follows Viv."

"Unbelievable," said Grace.

"It's true."

"Prove it."

"Let's have another demonstration. In this house tomorrow night," said Maggie, wiggling in curtains, as if preparing to break free.

"When will this ever end?" asked Ruby. "I'll allow no séances in my house."

"If you don't, Miss Turner, then we'll never leave." Maggie insisted on a final séance in the boardinghouse. Maggie promised that she and Valerie would leave forever, never to return to Concord, once the séance was complete. But only if the séance took place in Ruby's boardinghouse.

"If this is what it takes to get rid of you, I agree to host a séance here tomorrow night," said Ruby.

7.

The next evening, the boardinghouse filled with Spiritualists dressed in mourning. The final séance was to begin after an early supper. As twilight windows grew dark, Ruby's parlor filled with more guests, many strange women wearing widow's weeds. Dressed in deep mourning, all enjoyed dessert and coffee. They devoured a plate of bonbons near the toasty light of hearth flames.

Chris Datchery arrived, pushing Valerie Usherwood from Henry's house to Ruby's boardinghouse in the wheelchair. Sampson followed, helping Maggie, arms once again tied. Deftly, with one hand, he untied her near the parlor doorway. Ruby watched Maggie and Sampson argue in hushed voices. Chris wheeled Valerie toward the library.

"Understand," said Ruby, "no one else can know."

"The devil knows," said Maggie.

"How comforting," said Ruby.

"Chris and I will help prepare the library for the demonstration," Sampson said.

Despite her doubts, Ruby agreed to participate in the séance because she was curious to witness the outcome. She hoped to uncover the truth behind the twins' deceit. Why had they invaded her home and what did they hope to gain by tormenting Lara's daughters? Ruby twisted her strands of pearls into a noose, not realizing what she was doing.

"Ready," Sampson said, reaching out to help Ruby from her chair. They walked into the dark library with the Hayden sisters following Henry, Nick, and Jerry.

"Welcome," said Maggie, drawing the library's heavy brocade curtains to choke out the light of the moon. Now, it was too dark for Ruby to see anyone's face. She grasped Sampson's hand, worried she might fall. From every direction, she heard whispering, many voices.

"Silence," a woman announced while lighting only a few dimmed lamps.

Henry introduced the twins to the audience. "May I present the famous Spiritualists, Valerie and Maggie Usherwood? Born in Tennessee, they have levitated in iron cages in the châteaus of Paris and entered infamous circles of experimenters in Rome."

"Frauds," Sampson Redlaw said, disguising his utterance as a cough.

Pure entertainment, thought Ruby. Hogwash. But sinister. Still not a believer, in spite of the cries she had heard from the empty room, she suspected séances were a way to seduce the fragile into parting with money. She couldn't help but picture her sister as Ruby regarded her brother with pity, realizing he was the perfect victim.

Sampson Redlaw whispered to Ruby, "Let's catch them."

Ruby was grateful her eyes slowly adjusted to the dim light.

"Weep into glass," Maggie said, offering Ruby a glistening tear bottle. A beautiful tradition. Quite poetic. But this wasn't a funeral, Ruby reminded herself. What were the twins doing, toying with so many fragile emotions? The tear vials reminded Ruby of funerals she would rather forget— young soldiers, her mother's suicide so shortly after her father's death from tuberculosis, long after they had separated, long after they had last seen each other, as if they still loved each other all that time and were connected spiritually. Then, she remembered bitterly that she had not been invited to Lara's, Jon's, or Clara's funerals. She had no lachrymatory for them.

"A weeping vial for the lady?" Maggie approached Florence Green and then led Ruby to a stage decorated with spent hourglasses.

"The séance begins?" asked Ruby, sick of what she told herself was nonsense, though many guests were already weeping, their tears falling into vials.

"Death will reunite us all," said Maggie. "There's no reason to be afraid, Miss Turner."

"I'm not afraid," Ruby said, tossing her vial on the rug. It rolled and spun, landing at Michael Hayden's neatly polished shoes.

"Forgive me," Ruby said, surprised Michael was present.

"Dying is homecoming," said Maggie.

Ruby noted several men wearing black crepe bands on their left arms. Some wore black stoles, sashes, and shoulder scarves.

"Sheltered, safe from sorrow." Maggie said, reaching out to clasp her sister's wheelchair and handing Henry ropes to tie Valerie before facing the guests, gathered around her in audience. "You are here because of desire. Morbid desire!"

"Having lost children, husbands, sons, and brothers," Maggie continued, "friends, sisters, mothers, and lovers, you've spent so much time—countless hours—sitting in mausoleums."

Ruby dug her heels into the rug.

"Those who can afford it have purchased metal coffins with glass plates for viewing corpses' faces," said Maggie. "Those with more means have purchased coffins with two glass panes for viewing the entire body. But what good has it done? What have you seen? Has it comforted you or brought you solace, even joy, to watch the dead decay?"

"No," several voices called out beneath veils.

"I think not," Maggie said. "Looking into the casket brings misery until you are jealous of the undertaker."

"Look around this room," she ordered. "Some of you visit tombs on a regular basis. Others have opened the coffin to gaze upon the remains of your beloved. You have begged, crying for your husbands to dig your children from their graves—one last time. So you can hold them, behold them once more. Some of you have come to me, asking for my help, after begging your fathers to dig your husbands from the ground so you can see them again."

The women in widow's weeds began to wail, clutching at each other and their vials of tears.

"You know who you are by what you can't stop doing."

One of the women began to screech beneath her veil. The other widows attempted to restrain her. Maggie continued her accusatory speech, taking on the instructive tone of a religious orator during popular conversations at Concord's Town Hall.

"You're always taking one last look," said Maggie. "Afterward, you want to see more, but there isn't more. You look and keep looking, again and again, always saying it's the last time. Eventually, something changes—the face, farther and farther away, becoming something else, a mask, stranger each time you enter the tomb, each time you open the casket to gaze upon it. Covered with decay, with worms, it becomes another thing, not the one you knew."

Another wail from the widows, gathering together, more than one now screaming as hands attempted to cover mouths beneath black veils.

"Soon the beloved's face isn't a face," hissed Maggie. "All you see is decay. Each time you open the coffin, you're just watching edges retreat. Hollowing skin pulling away from teeth and eyes. Bones rise, hair and nails growing, haggard, as the body bloats and deflates, oozes, and shrinks away."

"Valerie and I have seen so many corpses. We know all the stages of decay. But what about the soul? Isn't the soul more than the body?" Maggie staggered, falling toward the table, catching herself on Nick Dalton, his expression horror.

"Rest, darling, rest," said Maggie, wheeling Valerie to

the far corner of the room.

"We will meet again." Maggie snuffed out the first lamp on a pathway to cover the parlor in darkness. "There shall be no night, only darkness." She extinguished other lamps.

Ruby wondered why women would choose to spend entire lives in mourning. She had tried so hard to remove herself from these sadnesses. By the light of the last lamp glowing, she glimpsed four in black veils united in fresh mourning, huddling in the far corner, near the cabinet, tucking tear vials beneath their veils. They wore widow's weeds so dense Ruby could not view their faces. Beneath weeping veils, wrapped in black gowns of crusted crepe, worn, aged in extreme wear, they clutched hair in shadow boxes. Sculpted into crosses and roses, human hair jewelry matched weeping willow brooches.

"Before we begin," said Maggie, lighting a single candle and offering it to the guests. "I give you all permission to examine the cabinets."

Taking the candle, Ruby used it liberally as Maggie followed.

Henry looped cord around Valerie's dainty waist. He then wrapped cord around her wrists, chest, ankles, and neck.

Sampson Redlaw examined the ligatures.

Guided by a single lamp, demi-flame veiled by a blue transparency, the guests gathered in a semi-circle, beginning and ending at the spirit cabinet. All hands joined a chain. After some minutes, Ruby heard the childlike mating cry of an owl. When Maggie announced the approach of a spirit, Sampson burst out laughing.

"Who's that?" Ruby asked.

"Valerie Usherwood!"

"What?"

"Listen to me!"

"Valerie?"

"We need order, not chaos. Silent sympathy, no

conversation."

Now it was dark, so dark. Ruby couldn't see Valerie, yet her voice was the same as Maggie's.

Maggie Usherwood entreated all to cooperate. "Silence," she said, "unless the spirit calls you to speak."

"How will we know?" Belle asked.

"Will Valerie tell us?" Aria asked.

"If all goes well, when she speaks," said Maggie, "she will no longer be my sister. A spirit will communicate through her. If she calls, it will be the spirit. Then, and only then."

"Meanwhile, what are we to do?" asked Grace.

"Just wait. Hope. And believe."

"Should we stop this?" Sampson asked, still holding Ruby's hand. As her eyes continued to adjust to the darkness, she focused on Maggie's face.

"No, no," Ruby answered, feeling her face flush when she realized Sampson had been addressing Grace.

Grace, rescuing her, said, "Quite right."

Maggie lit thirteen candles. In the light of the little flames, Ruby could see the furniture had been rearranged with the dining-room table in the library's center. On the table, something lumpy was covered by bedsheets. As Maggie slowly positioned candles around the edges of the table, Ruby could see a long funereal white sheet covered a body. Valerie? But how was it possible? Ruby had seen Henry tie Valerie to her wheelchair. Maggie moved the candles closer to the covered body, now distinct under the sheet as if unclothed. Ruby could make out ribs and toes, nose and mouth, the sheet moving as the body breathed.

Maggie said, "Gather before. Hold hands, forming a chain." At the head of the table, Maggie linked hands with Jerry and Nick. "Think kindness, and welcome."

Ruby held her breath, grasping Sampson's hand as she sensed his body stiffening. She glanced behind her and realized how cruel it was that Maggie had required them all to stand around the table, holding hands, as Sampson only had one hand to hold. How would he negotiate this?

Ruby craned her neck to glimpse the person standing on Sampson's left. Grace Hayden. Grace calmly reached for Sampson, her hand resting in the crook of his elbow. When Sampson turned to Ruby, he appeared to be smiling.

Maggie called to the ceiling, "Welcome, welcome! Come! We will hear. We will answer."

Ruby studied the faces lit by candlelight. Because of the position of the candles, the light illuminated mouths and chins, shadowing upper features, eyes cloaked in eerie guise with shadows like bruises.

"Come in. Come," Maggie said.

The table shook violently.

"Hold on!" Maggie said. "Don't let go. Don't break the circle."

The body under the sheet shot up. Sitting bolt upright on the table, still covered by the sheet, it dampened with a pool of saliva emphasizing the oval of a mouth. Wide open, the jaw unhinged as the figure drooled and gasped.

"Who are you?" Maggie asked.

No answer.

"Hello," Maggie said.

No answer.

"Welcome," said Maggie. "Please state your name."

"Lara Hayden," the voice said.

To Ruby's horror, she recognized the voice.

Ruby heard the Hayden sisters gasp. Belle cried out. The faces of Grace and Viv resembled stone caryatids. Aria attempted to stifle her cries, a choked lullaby.

"Lara?" Ruby asked.

"Don't break the circle," Maggie ordered.

Belle twisted away and Jerry held her while Nick comforted Aria.

"If you let her go, you know what will happen," Maggie

warned.

Jerry turned to Belle, his face bent down to hers, whispering so Ruby couldn't hear the words.

"Welcome, Lara," Maggie said. "Whom would you like to speak to?"

"Ruby?"

Ruby wanted to run. Sampson's grasp tightened over her hand.

Maggie said, "She's right here. You may speak to her."

"Help me be free. I want to escape," the voice under the sheet spoke. "Help, Ruby."

Ruby's ankles began to give way. Sampson held her up as she crumpled like a cloth doll, collapsing onto him. The voice faded, sounding farther and farther away, as if lost in a tunnel. "If I leave you, will you forgive me?"

The voice went silent, the body seized under the sheet before collapsing upon the table with a sickening thud.

Maggie said, "I need your hands to hold Valerie down so she won't hurt herself. Hurry. Hold her. She's coming back."

Under the sheet, Valerie convulsed like a mental patient in the violent ward. Aria had seen this before. Could this be what Valerie also suffered from, or was Valerie's affliction a gift? Aria wondered how one told the difference between a gift and a curse? Her love for music was like this, her greatest gift, her greatest affliction.

"Mother," Aria said, reaching the table. "Mother, please! Talk to me. Mother!"

"Lara's gone," Maggie said, as Nick stroked Aria's shoulder. "It's time for Valerie to come back. She can't share her body forever."

Sampson asked, mocking Maggie, "Might she accidently give her body away? Rent it out, like a room?"

"Mr. Redlaw, please. You would know more about women who offer their bodies for rent—likely more than anyone else in this room."

Maggie darted behind Grace.

Belle, crouching in a corner of the library, huddled in a ball, tucked into herself like a cat. Grace stared at the white sheet covering Valerie.

Aria began to draw back the sheet. Was Valerie breathing? The sheet was cold, so cold, as if taken from an ice box.

"Wait." Maggie pushed Aria away from the table, repositioning the sheet securely over Valerie's body and face. Maggie's hands circled Valerie from head to toe, as if trying to warm her, wake her, reanimate her. Henry and Ruby Turner attempted to pull Maggie off her sister. Maggie flung her arms at Henry, who cradled her against his bloated belly. She fought him and extinguished the lamp.

"Dr. Burrows?" asked Maggie.

The room was so dark now, so dark. But Aria could almost make out something by the moonlight from the window: Valerie's lips, painted gleaming pomegranate, her powdery skeletal heart-shaped face cracked like an old doll's face, her scaly skin tattooed with garlands of poppies and ivy, partly cloaked in drab, thistle-dark hair. Donning silver grapevine bangles twisted around bruised wrists, Valerie flashed a toothy frozen smile, fanglike. Her exposed incisors exuded delicacy and belligerence. Her mouth shot open. Blood began to drip from her tongue and her cracked lips. A trail of entrails bubbled from her mouth before slithering onto the dining-room table. They sloshed onto the sheet, now red with blood. Entwined at the end of the entrails, a padlock and key dropped from her open mouth.

"My sister has birthed another mystery," said Maggie, covering Valerie fully with the sheet, again, and holding up Ruby's missing skeleton key and a bloody padlock on a chain. Smiling as if the bleeding padlock were a dazzling jewel, Maggie winked at Viv, who recognized the padlock. Maggie held it dripping over her breast as she demonstrated

195

the skeleton key fit the padlock.

Maggie unlocked the padlock and Viv began to weep as a cacophony of ghosts sprang forth, uncaged from the darkness. Viv saw her mother and her father reaching out to her. She saw Godfrey appear and then disappear in shadows. She saw others: a woman who looked like Ruby followed by a series of lovely twin girls skipping and holding hands, laughing as if it were all a game to them.

Screams echoed in so many voices. Hundreds and hundreds of voices of men, women, and children screaming from another room in the house. At first, the screams were so terrifying that no one said anything. They just remained still, staring into each other's eyes. Viv felt warm liquid gushing between her legs, soaking her gown. It fell in heated rain on her shoes. Had anyone noticed? She was ashamed, so ashamed, and grateful for the darkness.

"The parlor," Sampson finally said. "Come, follow me."

Sampson ran, and the group ran after him, toward the screams as they moved through the house.

Viv was caught in the rush of her sisters dragging her along. The screams stopped and then began again. The screams of the children were the worst for Viv to endure. When she heard babies crying, she realized she hadn't wet herself the way she thought. Her water had broken.

Inside the dark parlor, screams resounded from every corner as the room was filling with numerous apparitions. The guests of the final séance scattered from the screams and then became emboldened when Sampson led them on a chase. Men and women were running to the screams, as if playing a game with spirits. The cacophony of ghost screams grew.

The voices led the guests to the dining room where they found the corpse preserver. Peering through its porthole window at the corpse inside, the guests were startled to see the corpse's face constantly changing to the faces of the guests.

The porthole window revealed dead faces of the living who were in the room. All those who attended the séance that night saw their own corpse face through the porthole window of the corpse preserver. The guests knew they would soon be dead and yet not even the knowledge of their deaths could make spirits quit laughing. Soon, the guests were laughing too, laughing at the faces of each other's corpses through the porthole window.

During the chaos, Viv hid her soaked gown. Realizing she was about to give birth, Viv was afraid to tell anyone. The entire room began laughing except for her. It was hysterical, but without humor. Viv clutched herself, hunching over, bracing against contractions that grew more powerful. Stumbling, she felt such pain as the contractions began again, coming faster, lasting longer. She tried not to moan as she felt herself opening.

At first, Viv suspected no one noticed her but then Willa emerged from a cabinet and began to crawl toward Viv while wearing a dark veil. Viv had another contraction, this one so sudden and terrible that she began to cry out. Willa placed a hand over Viv's mouth just as the wind blew the windows open and a magnificent bridelike white-veiled apparition appeared from behind the curtained windows. The bride began wailing into moonlight in the far corner of the parlor and howling at any guest who dared approach her.

The bride grew wings, enormous white wings to match her gown, as Viv's contractions grew stronger and closer together. More veiled apparitions gathered around her.

Willa led Viv to an isolated corner, behind the screaming ghost bride, which Viv now thought might be an angel. In the isolated corner, Godfrey waited in the white wings of the bride.

Viv hunched behind Godfrey as Willa held her, the three of them hidden and sheltered in the ghost bride's enormous white wings unfurling as Viv began pushing and pushing with Willa and Godfrey holding her hands. Thanks

197

to the drama of the séance and the mediums' theater, no one seemed to notice Viv squatting and panting. As she pushed, people were watching the bridelike apparition's turmoil as her wings began flapping to slap people's faces, flinging those who came too close.

While Godfrey and Willa sheltered her, Viv wondered if perhaps the others in the room saw Godfrey as another guest in the darkness. Willa, removing the veil from her face, guided Viv through her pain. The baby crowned beneath Viv's gown and Willa quietly held Viv's hand, encouraging her. With Willa's help, Viv tried to finish giving birth without making a sound.

The séance was a great distraction, full of moaning and howling as more apparitions appeared in the library. People ran to follow the spirits. It seemed as if several apparitions were working with Godfrey and Willa in conspiracy as Viv felt the baby pushing through her body, tearing her apart.

Every time Viv couldn't help but cry out in pain, Godfrey made a signal with his hand and the ghost bride began flapping her wings as if to take flight, filling the parlor with wind to make the curtains rise and women's hair whip above their heads in snarls. The ghost bride began to wail and moan and scream and then other apparitions joined her in a chorus of screaming, drowning out Viv's voice as Viv wept and moaned.

A new materialization had begun in the dark library. The bridelike apparition was giving birth to a spirit in the form of an owl with a human face as Viv was giving birth to Godfrey's child.

Once Viv's baby was born, Willa held the baby up but Viv could barely even see it glistening in the shadowy light. Instead, the brightly glowing human-faced owl flew into Viv's arms. Just before Viv passed out, she saw Godfrey and Willa holding her baby. She realized it was their baby—never hers. Willa and Godfrey slipped out of the room with the baby and no one else seemed to notice as the human-faced owl stared into Viv's eyes before taking flight.

* * *

After discovering Viv had fainted in a corner, Ruby lit a lamp and shone it on the parlor's bloody rug near Viv. "This demonstration has ruined Viv's gown," Ruby called out, standing upon afterbirth. "Someone assist her." Grace and Aria rushed to Viv. Viv began to stir and her eyes fluttered as Florence and Kora stared at her placenta in horror.

All around Viv was afterbirth speckled with white feathers dotted in blood.

"I'm alright. I'm fine," Viv said to her sisters, who helped her stand. "The apparition only frightened me when it stained my dress."

Ruby guided the lamplight over a body on the fainting couch. It was covered by a blood-drenched sheet. But Maggie took the lamp from Ruby and extinguished its flame. "The apparition," Maggie yelled, "requests permission to speak."

The chaos halted and the room got so quiet that the guests could hear the apparition whisper to Ruby, "What I am now, you soon will be."

"An abomination?" asked Michael Hayden.

"Seeing once knowing," the apparition said, her bloody hand reaching for Michael's hand as he stepped away.

Another voice came into the room, a male voice Ruby didn't recognize, her eyes scanning dark corners.

"Who does he look like?" asked Nick.

"A murder victim," said Maggie, "blood runs down his mouth as he speaks the name of his murderer."

"His murderer?" Nick asked. "Is he here?"

In the dark, Ruby sensed the apparition regarded her with curiosity, and Ruby sensed in her something that reminded her of a specter—the haggard, fixed, glassy

199

expression, under the translucent veil. Lara? Clara? Laughing with bosom heaving beneath the sheet, the apparition seemed to say, "I am happy to see my murderer among you."

Ruby gasped.

The apparition spoke in tremulous whisper, "I cannot yet go far away from my medium." As if sensing she was not fully understood, she repeated her words with infantile impatience. Making little coquettish signs, smiling, in a low tone, the apparition then addressed Henry. She asked Henry's name, then disappeared on the other side of the curtains. Ruby heard furniture moving.

Lighting a tiny candle, Henry asked to be favored with the sight of the apparition's foot, and she gracefully revealed herself again, stepping out from behind the curtains as she lifted her robe to the knee. Henry stroked her foot, which Ruby thought resembled that of an antique statue, white, plump, high and arched, yet cold, sculpted. Henry stroked the toes as if he had never seen a woman's foot before. Perhaps, he hadn't, thought Ruby, appalled to see her brother lost in the madness of the flesh. Ruby was gratified to witness Henry's shocked terror when the foot came off the woman's body. He held it with the severed ankle dripping blood on his hands.

Seeming affronted, the apparition took her foot away from Henry and then gathered the veil about her head, making sure to never reveal her face.

Sampson Redlaw addressed rude words to the apparition and Maggie attempted to wake Valerie with a song. The song demagnetized Valerie and the apparition, disappearing back into the cabinet.

A voice claiming to be Valerie invited Henry into the cabinet, asking Henry to make sure her hands and feet were satisfactorily secured. Henry fastened the string around her waist and then held it like a leash as he stepped outside the cabinet.

"What happened to the other?" asked Sampson. "The

cord Henry tied her up with earlier? And why doesn't she need her wheelchair now? Who is that under the sheet on the table?"

Ruby soon heard voices, as if Valerie were carrying on a conversation with some unknown person. Suddenly, the cabinet filled with light. Male and female faces appeared at the aperture of the cabinet. Among them was Lara. The light increased the color of Lara's eyes and lips.

The light extinguished and a new apparition with a luminous body advanced while allowing people to touch her violet hair.

This new apparition seated herself among the visitors and allowed them to touch her hands and feet as a delicious floral scent filled the parlor. She lay down on the rug so Henry could examine her. She laughed, eyes rolling in their sockets as Henry held her knees.

"Grab her legs," he said to Ruby, "before she goes into convulsions."

Henry trembled violently, staring at the white substance on his hands as he reached up to stroke the apparition's veil.

"I saw a great white ape behind Mr. Dalton," said Florence. "Look at the curtain, how it swells."

Ruby hoped to keep hold of Maggie, to monitor her movements. Maggie, in the form of the woman apparition, began to heave, vomiting string from her white veils. Pale liquid gushed from between her legs and from her mouth, covering her body like a wedding gown oozing and dribbling blobs of what appeared to be offal in foam.

What flowed from her veil appeared to be saliva cradled in delicate satin webbing. Ruby grabbed it, limp and sticky. She unthreaded the slippery webbing to discover flabby little limbs, twitching. She shivered, flicking it from her hands, wiping her fingers on the tablecloth. She withdrew a handkerchief from her dress pocket. Maggie, still in a trancelike state, tore off all her veils to reveal liquid exuding from her mouth as her face became a garish mask of pain. She grunted low and groaned, hunching on the rug, lurching, squatting while giving birth to a sound like a baby crying. As the cry faded, the apparition crawled back into the cabinet, where Valerie supposedly waited. The door closed and the room collapsed into a complete silence.

"What now?" Sampson asked finally, staring at the cabinet when the demonstration was over.

Everyone waited, staring at the cabinet doors as they closed.

When Henry finally opened the cabinet, no one was there.

Both of the twins were gone.

"But, where are they?" Ruby asked.

"I don't know," said Sampson. "They must have got away when we weren't looking."

"But how?" Ruby asked, looking around the room at her mystified guests. "We were all watching them."

The remaining guests looked at each other dumbfounded and it took several moments before Ruby realized she was clutching her skeleton key.

8.

The next day, as Ruby attempted to clean up the chaos of the night before, she discovered something so disturbing wrapped inside a soiled handkerchief. She was glad Henry visited. When he inspected it, he claimed it was a dematerialized hand.

"Dematerialized?" asked Ruby. "It's not a dematerialized hand. It's a real hand. Can't you see? Can't you smell? It's a woman's severed hand, rotting!"

"Maybe it is. That doesn't change the miracle of the twins."

"What do you mean?"

"Don't you see?" asked Henry. "Maggie's thoughts, the spirits' memories, take shape in Valerie through materializations. She's a developer of images from beyond the veil. Maggie is photographer, like Viv, but Valerie is her camera. A human camera. Materializations are their photographs. Maggie's mind locates three-dimensional images of the spirit realm, using Valerie's body to develop the images."

Inside the parlor curtains stained from the séance, Ruby discovered something resembling a flesh carving in the shape of a fetus. "I need to show this to the doctor," she said to Henry, and they took it to Dr. Burrows for him to examine.

"Let me see," Dr. Burrows said. "Clever girls, very clever, if they don't accidently kill themselves or someone else."

"What do you mean?" asked Ruby.

"The danger of a rotting hand is obvious. There is a reason why we bury our dead," said Dr. Burrows.

"But what of this oddity?"

"A carving, made of organic materials. The lung of a cow or another animal, an organ carved to resemble human

203

hands, the tissue sculpted."

Needing time to think, Ruby asked, "Is there something medically wrong with the twins?"

"The illusion requires them to force things in and out of their bodies, where certain things should not go. One of these days, they'll pay the ultimate price for what they've done to their bodies for the entertainment of their audience, if they haven't already."

"That's something to really be afraid of," said Ruby, banishing all thoughts of phantoms or spirits and confronting something much more troubling: young girls birthing dream figments and mirage impressions. But where did these chimeras come from and at what cost to the twins?

Ruby realized there might have been no ghosts or apparitions at the séance but rather something much more disturbing. Two unfortunate young girls had birthed malicious visions. Like a camera and photographer, the twins recorded, developed, and exposed whatever evil images they saw inside their audience.

9.

A week after the final séance, the boardinghouse had been cleaned and put back in order. The Hayden sisters had immediately approached their uncle, Michael Hayden, the following day and begged him to help them find a way to leave Ruby's boardinghouse. He was all too pleased to assist, no questions asked.

Michael used church connections to secure places for Viv, Grace, Belle, and Aria in a training program for school mistresses in Boston. The sisters agreed to leave Concord and to attend the training program while hoping to find teaching positions until they married suitable husbands.

Though Belle planned to wed Jerry in summer, she would accompany her sisters until Jerry built a house in Concord. Having promised it would be a fine house to raise children one day, Jerry promised to build it with the help of Sampson, Chris, and Nick.

Sampson begged to be allowed to visit Grace in Boston and Grace told him he may if Chris would accompany him to visit Viv.

Nick and Aria vowed to keep a long-distance musical connection by co-writing songs through a correspondence of unfinished lyrics. They promised they would sing these songs together when Nick accompanied Sampson and Chris on visits to Boston.

After all these promises were made, the Hayden sisters prepared to leave Ruby's boardinghouse. Viv's cameras and equipment had to be carefully boxed and sent ahead to Boston. Chris was helpful in this. Though typically concerned with her cameras, Viv seemed distracted.

The morning the Hayden sisters were to leave Ruby's boardinghouse in the silence of snowfall, Aria noticed Viv acting strangely. When they were gathering their final belongings in their rooms, Viv asked Aria if she heard a baby crying and a soft lullaby singing from the ceiling and walls. Viv claimed the singing was the most enchanting lullaby she had ever heard.

"Viv," said Aria, packing her bag, "quit fooling around. We're going to miss our train."

"Viv, hurry. Viv, come on!" Belle and Grace called after descending the boardinghouse stairs while Nick, Sampson, Jerry, and Chris carried their luggage out of the boardinghouse. Waiting for Viv and gazing back at the stairs, Belle, Grace, and Aria watched Viv lagging behind. Finally, the Hayden sisters exited the boardinghouse.

Outside in the snow while walking to the carriage where the men loaded the luggage and Belle and Grace waited, Aria turned and saw Viv staggering farther behind. Viv clutched her belly, stumbling.

Lurching down the snowy lane, away from the boardinghouse and toward the carriage that would drive them to the train station, Viv wasn't looking ahead but was looking back at the boardinghouse.

Aria tried to see what Viv was staring at—something high up in an upstairs boardinghouse window. Aria looked and looked, until she glimpsed people she had never seen in the boardinghouse: a man and a woman cradling an infant near the window of a room she didn't know existed.

10.

With no remaining boarders and feeling very much alone, Ruby rested her eyes at night in her boardinghouse with its many vacant rooms. She felt as if she kept hearing voices, a man and a woman talking upstairs and a baby crying. She knew that couldn't be right. Kora was up there, sleeping alone.

Ruby's eyes ached. Dry eyes and blurring vision were among the worst aspects of growing older for her—losing the crispness around the edges, especially at night. As the world dimmed and faded, her memories became vivid. Her childhood nearing in these moments, she saw Clara's face, again. It was her own face as a child, the face she had seen in mirrors.

"Clara," Ruby whispered, "Clara."

"Ruby?"

Ruby heard her name as a whisper—a woman's voice. She opened her eyes and turned toward where she heard it.

"Who's there?" Ruby asked. Her eyes scanned every corner of her bedroom. She saw no one but noticed photographs scattered over her bed—images of her and Clara as children.

In the photographs, the twin girls were young and bright-eyed innocents in the big ballroom of the plantation. But how did the photographs get there? There were no photographers in the plantation taking pictures of her and her sister in those days. They had no photographs of the plantation then. None of her and Clara as girls. She would have remembered. How, she wondered, did these photographs of her and her twin as children get here? She stood, thinking, trying to remember. The longer she stared at the images, the more she realized they had to be photographs of two other twin girls at the plantation—Valerie and Maggie. Valerie and Maggie looked so much like Ruby and Clara. Of course, they all had the same great-grandfather.

It confused her to think of her family. All these lives forever connected in chaos through marriage and slavery. No one would talk about how they looked just like each other— Valerie and Maggie and Clara and Ruby, the girls they once had been. Or, perhaps, no one could see it but Ruby? Was this why she never wanted to be near Maggie and Valerie, didn't want them living in her boardinghouse, didn't want to try to find matches for them, and asked Henry to lock them away? Was it possible—that she didn't want to save the twins because they reminded her of who she once was?

She gazed into her oval mirror and found her eyes harsh now, like Clara's eyes.

Perhaps because of the scattered photographs, other details of the room seemed off. Ruby surveyed every detail— the dried roses in their tall green vases, the candelabra, violet and crystal perfume bottles, the bed with its oversized canopy, the heavy tattered bible on her nightstand, a landscape painting in oils of the old plantation where she and Clara were born, where she and Clara used to play with captive children like dolls. It was hard to imagine such a childhood for a fierce abolitionist like her.

"Ruby?"

"Who's there?"

The chair near the vanity table sat in an odd position, twisted away from the oval mirror. She wondered if Kora had moved it while cleaning. The burgundy rug had been recently swept, and yet seemed different. Odd. Ruby bent down to stroke the soft fluffy rug with her fingertips and noticed parallel lines imprinted deeply.

"Ruby?"

Her blood running cold. Ruby began to crawl along

the rug, slowly gazing beneath her bed and seeing only the shadow of ruffles. She crawled to look beneath the vanity, behind the plush divan, beneath it.

"Ruby?"

Slowly, Ruby rose. Resting on her aching knees, she stared at the closet. Someone, she thought, hid behind the door, nestled in her gowns while whispering her name. Just like when she was a girl, at the family plantation, when she and Clara used to play hide-and-seek with the other children.

"Ruby?"

They played this game all the time, until one little girl got lost and was never found. Mother was so unhappy and forbade Ruby and Clara to ever play the game again. Shortly after blue mold grew near the putrid smell behind the cubby of the ballroom stairwell, their parents separated.

"Ruby?"

Ruby's gaze moved over the bed, behind the bed, over the vanity, to the mirror, where she saw it—in the far corner, the bulge in the heavy brocade curtains over the windows that led out to her sleeping porch. She froze, steadying her nerves. She clinched her fists and walked toward the curtains.

"Ruby."

The bulge was short, boxy, squat. Ruby touched the rough fabric of the curtain ever so gently and pulled it back. She gasped to see Valerie's wheelchair. Ruby attempted to pull the wheelchair out of the curtains but it was stuck. She rustled the curtains, shaking them out of the chair's spokes, pulling at the curtains. That's when she noticed an aged, fire-scarred hand holding the wheelchair tightly in place. Hiding behind the curtains, clutching the wheelchair, a woman crouched in heavy mourning—her long black dress, black hat and black veil covering her face and neck.

The woman shoved the wheelchair into Ruby, knocking her onto the bed. The veiled woman closed the bedroom door as Ruby stared at the knob in her mangled hands. Too shocked to scream, Ruby bent to the strength of the strange woman.

"Sit down, sister," the woman said, forcing Ruby into the wheelchair.

Ruby began to shake, unable to respond.

"It's your turn to sit in the chair now," the veiled woman said, her face hidden in black lace.

Ruby was moved in the wheelchair. She watched helplessly as the woman walked through her room, going through her closet, laying out Ruby's clothes as if packing for a journey. The woman laid out one of Ruby's traveling dresses on the bed and Ruby's boots on the rug. The woman removed her hat and veil and turned so that Ruby saw her own face—Clara's face—smiling.

Clara undressed, removing her mourning attire to put on Ruby's dress and boots.

"Remember when we used to play this game?" whispered Clara. "Wasn't it fun?"

"No," said Ruby. She remembered the game well. She and Clara would trade places, trade clothes, trade beds, trade names, pretending to be each other. Their parents never knew. Only Henry and Jon suspected. Sometimes the game went on so long it was easy to forget who she was.

"Clara?"

"No, silly. I'm Ruby. You're Clara."

"Clara?"

"No. I'm Ruby."

"I'm Ruby."

"Remember?"

Clara, dressed in Ruby's clothes, laid out her mourning dress, hat, and veil on the bed.

Just like when she was a child, Ruby put on her sister's clothing. Clara led Ruby back to the wheelchair, where Ruby sat as Clara pulled the veil over Ruby's face.

Clara began to wheel Ruby through the dark

boardinghouse, quietly through the hallways, until the boardinghouse began to look strange to Ruby. Clara paused before a wall-length mirror, as if to give Ruby a view of herself. Clara pulled on the mirror. It opened like a door on hinges to reveal a room. Inside, by the light of thirteen candles burning, a dumb supper was in progress. Six women in widow's weeds, with faces hidden in black veils, all in deep mourning attire, sat at a dining table heavy with food, with the silverware reversed. Near them, a single empty plate was set but without a chair. Clara wheeled Ruby to the empty plate that seemed to have been reserved for her.

Clara left the room.

Without speaking or removing their veils, the women offered Ruby food and began to fill her plate. In silence, not wanting to offend her hosts, Ruby attempted to eat, but the food had no flavor. She found it difficult to swallow.

After a few moments, a man and woman entered the room, carrying an infant.

Ruby could not make out their faces by the dim light, but she had the distinct impression they could not see her or the women dining at the table. Ruby was suddenly hungry and began to devour the food on her plate in large bites, careless of her manners. Unladylike, greedily rushing the meal, she bit her tongue and dropped her fork onto her plate. The fork clattered, breaking the silence, splattering smashed potatoes.

At the sound, the women laughed as if they were crying. They wouldn't stop laughing or perhaps they couldn't.

The man and woman got up abruptly and left the room with the infant. The man closed the mirror door, shutting Ruby in with the women of the dumb supper.

Not knowing what to do and unable to find her bearings, Ruby stood up from the table and began tiptoeing around the room, touching all the women in the darkness. Disoriented by their laughter as it crested and ebbed in waves, Ruby dropped to her knees, crawling along the edges of the walls while searching for the door. She couldn't find it, though she went around and around the walls.

Exhausted, she finally crawled back to her place at the table. She sat in the wheelchair and prepared to eat again. As she lifted her fork to her lips, the women began to feast in silence, lifting their veils to reveal only shadows.

ACKNOWLEDGMENTS

Grateful acknowledgment is made to all who journeyed with me as I labored on, dreamed of, and was haunted by this novel for the past ten years.

I would like to thank the American Antiquarian Society for supporting the historical research through a William Randolph Hearst Creative Artists Fellowship.

I would also like to thank the North Carolina Arts Council for providing support for my writing in the form of an Artist Fellowship.

Finally, I would like to thank Jesi Buell and Patrick Parks for their readings of numerous drafts. Their editorial notes, suggestions, and detailed comments helped me through the final stages of revision when I was most in need of insight.

www.ingramcontent.com/pod-product-compliance
Lightning Source LLC
Chambersburg PA
CBHW050343030726
47503CB00008B/2590